HAL

The Third-Class Hero

HAL
The Third-Class Hero

SONIA CRADDOCK

HarperCollins*Publishers*Ltd

First Edition

Canadian Cataloguing in Publication Data

Craddock, Sonia
  Hal, the third-class hero

ISBN 0-00-647415-2

I. Title.

PS8555.R23H34 1992   jC813'.54   C92-094633-X
PZ7.C73Ha 1992

92 93 94 95 96 97 98 99 ❖ OFF 10 9 8 7 6 5 4 3 2 1

To Amy and Martyn

HAL
The Third-Class Hero

One

HERO FOR HIRE

Hal knew you had to get out of bed early if you were only a third-class hero looking for a job. There were a lot of third-class heroes (and heroines, too) and jobs went fast. Times really weren't what they used to be. There were so many heroes that they had wiped out most of the monsters and rescued most of the maidens that needed rescuing (as well as a lot that didn't). No, it was every hero for himself, reflected Hal, as he hurried along the street to the notice board in the town square.

Hal had been trying to get a job for nearly six months, ever since he'd graduated from Hero School. As it was, he'd barely graduated—he'd almost failed the hero exams and only got a third-class certificate.

The hero rules were very strict. First-class heroes got paid the most and were allowed to have two horses, a gold handled sword and a servant. Second-class heroes were allowed one horse and a sword with silver decorations. Third-class heroes got the lowest pay, no horse and a plain sword.

Hal frowned. It was slow work being a hero without a horse. For one thing, all the first- and second-class heroes got to the jobs first.

But this time, he thought, as he read the notice on the board, this time his luck might change.

King wants hero to rescue his daughter who has been seized by a sea serpent. All expenses paid plus bonus of twenty gold crowns for successful recovery of daughter (alive). Interested heroes apply at castle.

Hal noted that it was pretty poor pay and that the king hadn't mentioned which castle. But that was to be expected. Kings were notoriously cheap and they were such egotists that they forgot there were other kings and other castles around. He would have to spend some of his last few pennies on a crystal reading.

He made his way to the narrow street where the crystal reading shops were. You had to be careful how you picked one. Some of the claims the gazers made were just plain lies, and the cut-price bargains weren't to be trusted. His mother, one of the first heroines, had always said you got what you paid for, so Hal ignored a shop that advertised three gazings for the price of one and another that was giving away free cold charms, guaranteed to stop you sniffling for one hundred and fifty days. Hal wouldn't have minded a cold charm but heroes weren't supposed to have anything to do with magic. Even gazings were frowned on. He couldn't afford to be reported to the Heroes Committee and lose his hero certificate.

Hal's eye caught a sign. "Satisfaction Guaranteed. Mother Rosa's Crystal Readings." That sounded all right and he dived down the steps to the basement shop.

It was dark inside and Hal, in his long pointed hero boots, tripped over a cat and caught his sword in a curtain. "Hurry up," said a voice. "Time is money. Do you want one gazing or the special?"

"What's the special?" said Hal, untangling himself and sitting down on a chair in front of a large crystal globe.

"Today's special is a double reading for only twenty-five pennies," said Mother Rosa, who was sitting on the other side of the table.

"How much is one reading?" said Hal, who didn't have twenty-five pennies.

Mother Rosa sighed. She was shrouded in a black wool shawl, probably to keep warm as it was damp and chilly in the basement. "Ten pennies," she said, and held out her hand. "In advance." She'd had experience with third-class heroes before. They were supposed to be the soul of honor, but there were some bad ones who wouldn't pay for anything.

Hal counted out the ten pennies. This left him only five.

"There's a hero-wanted notice on the board in the town square," he said. "But it doesn't say where to go. Can you show me the place? It's a king's castle."

Mother Rosa grumbled. "That's really a two-step gazing," she sniffed. "You should have said."

"I didn't know," said Hal.

"Well, all right," said Mother Rosa resignedly. "Look into the crystal and count to two hundred." She waved her hands over the globe and it began to flash with light.

Hal stared. The light didn't seem very bright. "That's a very old-looking crystal," he said, suddenly worried. "Don't you have a better one?"

"No," said Mother Rosa. "This crystal was good enough for my grandmother. It was good enough for my mother and it's good enough for me. Now concentrate or you'll waste your money."

Hal sighed. He should have checked first. Now it was too late. He didn't have enough money to go anywhere else.

"Concentrate," snapped Mother Rosa.

Hal concentrated. He fixed his gaze on the crystal and began counting. At one hundred and nine, he was still seeing nothing but flashes of light. He

4

gritted his teeth and counted harder. At one hundred and fifty, he saw a picture growing inside the crystal. It was the notice board. He could read the words as clearly as if he were there in the town square. Then the picture faded and he counted grimly on. At one hundred and seventy-one, a second picture appeared. It was a white stone castle that had a red flag with orange stripes flying at the top of the tallest tower. That must be it, Hal thought as the picture faded, but something kept him counting on, and at one hundred and ninety, a third picture rose in the globe. It was another castle. From the top of the square granite tower a blue flag with small white circles waved gently.

"One hundred and ninety-nine, two hundred," Hal counted, and the light in the crystal snapped off.

"How come I saw two castles?" he asked, shaking his head. "I only wanted one."

"Some people are never satisfied," sniffed Mama Rosa. "You got three pictures for the price of one and you're complaining."

"But which castle is the right one?" said Hal crossly.

"How should I know? You're not paying me to interpret." And she wrapped her shawl more tightly around her.

Hal hit the crystal with his fist and walked outside. Now what?

He sat down on the sidewalk and pulled out his Hero Handbook. There was a page that showed all

5

the official flags and who they belonged to. He could at least find out where the castles were. The first one was easy. A red flag with orange stripes. It was the flag of King Maze and he lived at Castle Maze on the coast. The second one took longer to find. Blue seemed a popular color for flags. Kings and queens were always changing their flags to keep up with fashion. The year before, a lot of them had changed to yellow. And they were forever tearing down castles to build more fashionable ones.

Hal's finger stopped halfway down the page. There it was. A blue flag with small white circles. King Aristo of Castle High on High Mountain.

Hal tucked his handbook back into the leather satchel he carried on his back and considered the situation. The two castles were in opposite directions from the town. He couldn't afford to make a mistake. Already his stomach was rumbling with hunger and he had only five pennies left. Was it King Aristo or King Maze? He had one clue to go on. It had better be right.

Two

HAL MEETS TROUBLE

The advertisement for a hero said that a sea serpent had seized the princess. So Hal assumed the castle he was looking for must be near the sea. Therefore, the right castle had to be Castle Maze on the coast. Having made this decision, Hal took the coast road.

The road led south through peaceful lanes and vineyards. Hal walked as fast as he could, determined to be the first hero to get to Castle Maze. Rule #9 in the Hero Handbook said that the first hero to apply for a job had the best chance. Hal knew the rules very well. When he had nothing better to do, he studied them carefully.

Hal whistled as he walked along. Even if he

didn't actually manage to rescue the princess, the advertisement had said all expenses paid and that meant food! And with any luck he could spin the job out for a few months. Of course, the hero code of ethics said that heroes weren't supposed to keep a job going for longer than they needed to. But everyone did. It was a well known fact that even a first-class hero like Gregory the Grey had managed to keep the Duke of Lonely Lake feeding him for three years while he searched for a renegade unicorn, which of course he never found.

At this point, the lane crossed a small stream and Hal rested for a moment on the wooden bridge. He pulled out a dry crust of bread from his pack and chewed it slowly, wishing it were cold chicken instead.

It was a peaceful spot. The stream gurgled under the bridge, the banks were covered with flowers, and the sun shone warmly. Hal began to feel drowsy and started to yawn. And then, as his eyes rested on the long bullrushes along the edge of the stream, he saw a flutter of white. And then a cry came to his ears, a small pitiful cry.

Hal vaulted onto the railing of the bridge and stared across the stream. Something, or someone, was lying half in and half out of the water!

Hal cursed under his breath. Heroes were not supposed to curse, but just then he didn't care. He cursed again. If he went and rescued this creature, he'd lose time and some other hero would get to

King Maze first. But Rule #3 in the Hero Handbook stated that all creatures in distress should be helped.

Hal looked around carefully. The road was empty. No one would know if he didn't stop. Why should he stop and lose a job?

"Awoo!" The small cry drifted across the stream.

Hal sighed. Rules were rules. He'd have to go and have a look. Grumbling and muttering to himself about his bad luck, he jumped down from the railing and walked along the muddy bank of the stream towards the moaning creature. His red leather boots soon became caked in mud and soaked with water.

"Awooooo! Awooooo!" came the cry from the rushes.

"I'm coming," Hal called angrily, breaking through the rushes with his hands.

"Awooo!" came the pitiful cry again, and there in front of him was a bedraggled dragon hatchling, struggling to extricate itself from its cracked white shell.

Hal stopped dead in his tracks. "Oh no!" he whispered, and he flung his hand over his eyes. If the hatchling bonded to him, he'd never be rid of it. It would think he was its mother or father and follow him everywhere.

Dragons were a real nuisance. There were no wild ones left, but occasionally an old egg that had been left years before suddenly cracked open and a dragon hatchling was born. The people who found these dragons lived to regret it. The dragons grew and grew and ate and ate, and were never any good for anything, and they were always setting fire to the house. Dragons were not noted for their brains and were difficult to train. The best you could hope for was to use them for transportation, and even then they were unreliable and tended to drop people off when they flew upside down.

Hal approached the trapped hatchling with great caution. All he had to do was free it from the shell and then disappear without their eyes meeting. Let some other poor fool bond with the creature. There was nothing in the hero rules that said he had to take care of a young dragon.

Keeping one hand over his eyes, he cautiously grabbed the shell and began prizing it away from the creature. He'd never seen such a tiny dragon before. It was really pathetic, all wrinkled, with a head too big for its body.

The shell was as hard as iron and Hal puffed and panted as he tried to wrench it open. He closed his eyes and pulled with both hands. Finally, with one great tug, a large piece tore off, sending him tumbling backwards onto the muddy bank.

Hal's head hit the ground with a *whump!* that made the world spin dizzily round and round, and when he groggily lifted his head, the dragon was sitting on his chest, staring right at him with shining golden eyes.

"Ook!" it said, tipping its head to one side and

clacking its tiny beak. "Ook! Ook!" And it bounced up and down, digging its claws into his stomach.

"Ook!" said Hal hopelessly, as he struggled to sit up. "Ook to you, too." And he grabbed the tiny dragon and held it up in the air.

"All right, you hatchling. I'm not going to be stuck with you. I'll charm you, even if I am a hero."

Hal did have a charm, a spell that changed living creatures into rock. He had bought it cheap from a pedlar, who told him that it would come in handy if he were attacked by a dangerous monster. Of course, heroes were forbidden to use charms. Rule #31. But most third-class heroes kept a few for emergencies, and Hal was so angry about losing time that he didn't care what he did, as long as he could get moving.

Holding onto the dragon with one hand, he fumbled in his pack for the yellow papered package that contained the changing spell.

Three

DRAGON PIE

Hal waved his changing charm over the dragon's head and shook it hard. Nothing happened. The dragon just called out "Ook! Ook!" and laid its dirty grey beak lovingly against Hal's cheek. Then it closed its eyes and fell asleep.

Hal sighed and threw the changing spell away in disgust. No wonder the spell had been so cheap—it was probably stale. He was stuck with a dragon. What bad luck! The only thing he could do was to tuck the hatchling into his bag and hurry back to the road. If he moved fast and walked through the night, he could be at Castle Maze by dawn.

By the time dark came, Hal felt as if he had been

walking for years. He had a blister on one foot and he wished for the millionth time that he had a horse. A hero should have a horse. A hero should have a marvelous fast horse that could gallop through the night. He limped along the road, dreaming of horses with red bridles and golden manes. It was hard to be a third-class hero. His father had wanted him to be a juggler, there was good money in it. But he hadn't been able to juggle more than three balls at a time, so the juggling school had asked him to leave. He'd been lucky to be accepted into Hero School. If it hadn't been for his mother, a great heroine, they would never have taken him. If only he'd studied harder.

All at once, Hal's thoughts were interrupted by the smell of toasting cheese. His stomach did a lively dance inside him and his nose twitched. What a smell! Oh, he was so hungry!

It seemed to be coming from a small cottage at the side of the road. There was smoke curling out of its chimney and warm yellow light glowed at the windows.

Before he knew what he was doing, Hal had walked up to the front door and knocked loudly.

The door creaked open.

"Yes?" a small voice quavered. "Who are you, and what do you want?"

A dwarf peered out shortsightedly. He was dressed in a red and blue striped tunic and had comfortable-looking slippers on his feet. In one hand he held a fork with a piece of toasted bread and cheese stuck on it.

Hal's mouth watered. "I'm Hal, a third-class hero, and I wondered if I could buy some supper from you."

"Hmmm," said the dwarf, opening the door a little wider. "I've had experience with third-class heroes before. Have you any money?"

"Five pennies," said Hal, taking his bag off his shoulder. "Sir," he added, remembering that dwarves liked to be flattered.

He fumbled in his bag for the money, and the next moment he was dancing up and down, yelling, with the baby dragon hanging from his wrist, its sharp razor teeth sunk into his skin. "Get this pest off me," he shouted to the dwarf.

The dwarf shook his head slowly. "That's impossible," he said. "You know that. You must have frightened it. You'll have to wait until it calms down."

Hal gritted his teeth and shook the dragon with his other hand. But the dwarf was right. There was no way he could dislodge those teeth.

"You'd better come in," said the dwarf crossly. "I don't want you hanging around my doorstep screaming all night. The neighbors will think I'm up to something and goodness knows we dwarves have enough to put up with as it is. We're always being picked on."

He shut the door behind Hal and, grumbling away, led him into a small room where a bright fire was glowing and the smell of toasted cheese filled the air.

"Sit down by the fire," he said. "Maybe when it gets warm it will fall asleep and let go. Why anyone would want a dragon is beyond me, but then third-class heroes aren't so bright, are they?"

Hal knew better than to argue with a dwarf. They loved arguing and would go on for hours. So he said nothing and sat in a small chair pulled up by the fire, trying to ignore the pain of the dragon's teeth in his wrist.

After a few moments, the dragon began to relax, and its eyes, which had been blinking up and down furiously, began to close. Unfortunately, Hal's eyes did too. The warmth of the room after the cool of the spring night had a sleepy effect upon him, and both the dragon and Hal nodded off at the same time.

"Third-class heroes aren't so bright, are they," repeated the dwarf, grinning from ear to ear. "Oh dear, no, they aren't." And, with one swoop, he deftly scooped up the sleeping dragon, whose teeth had by now relaxed their grip on poor Hal's wrist.

"Dragon pie," he said, smacking his lips. "I haven't had that for years." Being careful not to wake up the hatchling, he put it inside a wooden chest and closed the lid. Then he turned his attention to Hal's leather bag.

He wasn't a bad dwarf, as dwarves go, but if third-class heroes go to sleep in your front room and leave their bags open on the floor, what do they expect?

There wasn't much in the bag. Five pennies, some plasters for sore feet, a binding charm, a vanishing charm (these made the dwarf sniff, for those sorts of charms rarely worked), a packet of teeth-cleaning gum, a clean tunic, a pair of clean hose, a comb, the Hero Handbook, and some very tired-looking wonder-drops. The dwarf popped one of these into his mouth and sucked. They were supposed to bring pictures of the wonders of the world into your head, but this drop just tasted stale. The dwarf spat it into the fire, and put the five pennies into his pocket.

At that moment, Hal woke up with a jerk.

"Thief!" he cried, and pulled out his sword and lunged at the dwarf.

"No! No!" The dwarf dodged backwards. "I was just looking."

"Liar!" Hal held the point of his sword against the dwarf's ample stomach, and with the other hand rummaged through his bag. "Where's my money?" he demanded.

The dwarf held out the five pennies. "I was, uh, going to get you something to eat. Five pennies worth."

"Liar!" said Hal again, prodding the dwarf with the point of his sword. "I can kill you for this, you know."

The dwarf backed away until he was nearly in the fire. "Please, no, spare me," he pleaded. "I'll give you supper free, if you do."

"Stealing from a hero is punishable by death," snapped Hal. "Rule #11. Do you want me to break the hero rules?"

"I'll make you a dragon pie," the dwarf said.

"Dragon pie!" Hal exclaimed. "You've taken my dragon, too!" In his anger, he forgot that he hadn't wanted the hatchling in the first place. "You know full well that a dragon is a protected beast. It's against the law for anyone but a hero to kill a dragon."

"Unless the hero gives it as a present," said the dwarf. He inched over to the carved wooden chest and pulled out the hatchling, being careful to hold it so its teeth couldn't get a grip on him.

The dragon woke up and squeaked, looking around for Hal. The dwarf let it go and it crawled and flapped its way across the floor and folded itself around Hal's legs.

"I never gave you anything," said Hal, and he waved his sword angrily and advanced on the dwarf.

Four

SECRETS

"Toasted cheese!" the dwarf said, hiding his face in his hands as the sword came closer. Hal gave a laugh and put the sword back in its sheath. "It's a good thing for you I'm hungry," he said. "Now toast that cheese or I'll give you a haircut you'll remember."

The dwarf breathed out in relief and began bustling round the room. "It would go faster if we could use your sword to toast the cheese," he said.

"My hero sword?" said Hal. "My sword is for daring deeds of glory, not toasting cheese!"

"Well, it would just be quicker," said the flustered dwarf, dropping bread on the floor.

"Oh, very well," said Hal, who was so hungry he

felt he couldn't wait another minute. And he took his sword out and skewered three lumps of cheese on the end of it and held them to melt by the fire.

"Ouch!" Hal dropped the sword and grabbed his hand. "The handle is red hot!"

"Heat travels through metal," said the dwarf, shaking his head and picking up the blackened sword with a potholder. "You should have wrapped something around it."

After this, all went well. Ten minutes later, Hal was sitting down to a good supper of toasted cheese, pickles, and homebrewed ale, and the dragon snuffled in front of the fire with a large bowl of bread and milk.

"Where are you going?" asked the dwarf, when Hal pushed back his chair with a contented groan.

"Castle Maze," he said. "The king's daughter has been kidnapped by a sea serpent and he wants a hero to rescue her."

The dwarf nodded. "I've heard about that," he said. "My cousin works in the castle." He was silent for a moment and then he continued. "Since you spared my life, I'll tell you something that may help you. King Maze is a real joker. You can't get to the castle from the land side without going through a giant maze. Hedges twenty feet tall and so thick they're impenetrable, even with a sword. People get lost for days. If you don't know the secret, you'll never get through and you'll have to wait for the king's men. Once a month they go through the whole thing and rescue all the lost people. The king thinks it's hilarious."

"Do you know the secret?" Hal asked anxiously.

The dwarf nodded. "My cousin told me. The secret number is seven. Every time you come to a fork, turn right, and on the seventh count you turn left. Then you continue turning left at each fork and on the seventh count turn right again. If you follow this pattern all the way, you'll get through to the middle with no trouble."

"Well," said Hal, as he tucked the hatchling dragon back into his bag and got ready to leave. "I'm glad I didn't kill you. Thank you. I'm much obliged."

"Here, take this with you." The dwarf rummaged in his belt pocket and pulled out a tiny wishbone. "My cousin's name is Celti. If you see him, give him this and tell him that Rolf sends him greetings and bids him help you."

Hal thanked him again, and then opened the door and disappeared into the dark of the road.

Although it was spring, the nights were cold and Hal shivered as he marched along. There was no moon and it was difficult to keep to the road, especially as it was not in good repair and at times was little more than a cart track. But he made steady enough progress until he came to a junction, a little before dawn.

"Bother," said Hal, seeing the fork in the road. "Which way now?"

He looked around and then saw an old signpost at the side of the road. It was still too dark to make out the words on the signpost easily, but after a while Hal deciphered the words, "Castle Maze 13 leagues" on the sign that pointed to the left.

"Good," he said, but then, just to be prudent, he looked at the sign that pointed to the right. "Castle Maze 3 leagues," he read. "Even better," he said, and turned to the right fork. "I'll be there before they serve breakfast."

As day dawned and the spring sun rose above the horizon, Hal spied the turrets of Castle Maze in the distance with the red and orange flag flying from the topmost tower, and his step quickened with the thought of hot food and drink.

But suddenly, as he turned a corner, the road stopped dead, and in front of him was a sea inlet with Castle Maze on the other side.

Hal stared at the rippling blue water. The sign had said three leagues, but it hadn't mentioned that two of them were so wet!

There was a muddy path winding through the reeds. Hal hurried along it. Maybe there was a ferry boat. But after a few twists and turns, the path stopped dead at a small reed hut that was almost hidden by banks of tall green bullrushes.

"Put your hands over your head!" a voice rang out from behind him. "If you touch your sword, I'll shoot."

Hal whirled around. Beside a clump of alder

bushes knelt a girl dressed in a ragged grey tunic. She was holding a strung bow and the arrow was pointing right at Hal's heart.

Hal slowly raised his hands above his head.

"That's better," said the girl, and she came forward warily. "Who are you and what do you want?"

"My name is Hal. I'm a third-class hero and I'm trying to get to Castle Maze," said Hal.

"Without a boat?" laughed the girl scornfully. "You'll get a bit wet!"

But she lowered her bow. "I have no name and I live here." She pointed to the reed hut. "I keep geese and ducks. Robbers used to try and steal them. They don't any more." She twanged her bow and grinned. "I shoot them dead." She said this very calmly as if it were an everyday affair.

Hal wondered why the girl had no name. It would be very awkward not to have a name. He had often wished for a longer one. Hal, he felt, was very short and not a proper name for a hero.

"Do you have a boat I could borrow?" he asked. "I have a few pennies to pay."

"I've a coracle," said the girl. "You can borrow that," and she held out a dirty hand for the money. Then she led the way around the reed hut to a backwater, where geese and ducks swam.

"There it is," she said proudly. "I made it myself."

"That's a boat?" said Hal, looking at the round reed basket tied up under a willow tree.

"All my own," said the girl.

Hal shrugged and walked around to the tree. "How does it work?" he said. He stepped into it and crouched inside with his knees hitting his chin.

"You use this," said the girl, giving him a small wooden paddle.

Hal put the paddle in the water and paddled hard, and the round coracle spun in a dizzy circle, coming to a stop next to a large gander who pecked Hal hard on the ear.

"Call off your bird!" yelled Hal.

"Jeremy! Come here," ordered the girl, and the gander cackled and waddled towards her.

Hal took a deep breath and tried the paddle again. This time, he spun in the opposite direction, cracked his chin on his knees, and ended up among a group of very surprised ducks.

The leader, a fine white bird with a golden chain around its neck, tried to climb into the coracle with him.

"Get out!" shouted Hal, as the coracle tipped and rolled. "Get out, you stupid bird!" But the duck panicked and moved forward instead, and the coracle spun around, pitched forward, and turned upside down.

Hal sank to the bottom, about six inches down, and sat in the mud, cursing horribly. Inside Hal's bag, the dragon had woken up and was hissing in fright. The duck who had caused the disturbance began quacking angrily.

"You stupid bird!" shouted Hal, and he wrenched the gold chain from its neck. "I'll take this. Why has a duck got a gold chain round its neck anyway?"

"Give that back, it's mine." The girl was leaning over the bank. "I let the ducks wear it for a day each as a treat. But it's mine. I had it when I was a baby."

Hal stood up, the mud dripping off him in black drops. "Be quiet!" he snapped at the dragon, who was whimpering plaintively, and then he examined the chain.

It was made of fine gold threads with a golden locket at the end. Hal pressed the catch on the locket and it sprang open. Inside was a miniature of a baby with black tangled curls. On the baby's head was a jewelled coronet, and there were some words in silver around the rim.

Princess Alta of Aristo, Hal read to himself. Now, where had he heard that name before? Quite recently, too. He shook his head impatiently. A hero should have a better memory.

"It's worth a lot of money," said Hal. "You should sell it and buy a decent boat."

"There's nothing wrong with my coracle," she snapped, "if you paddle it right."

Hal squelched to the shore and emptied the water from his boots. "I think I'll walk," he said. "It's safer."

"Suit yourself," said the girl.

"And I'll trouble you for my money back," said

Hal, "since I didn't use the boat."

The girl laughed. "You took the coracle and turned it upside down. Now I have to dry it. There's no way you'll get your money back. Fair's fair."

And before he could say a word, she had grabbed the coracle, turned it up the right way, and was paddling neatly across the water.

Hal shifted the dragon in the pack to balance the weight, and set off to the fork in the road where he had been led astray, his feet slopping in his soaking boots. What a waste of time that had been. He just hoped he wouldn't be too late.

Five

DANGER IN THE MAZE

Nothing seemed to be going right. First the dragon, then the dwarf. Then the wrong road, and then that silly boat that went in circles. He would be lucky if there weren't a hundred heroes at the castle before him now.

It was a foot-sore, damp, and weary third-class hero that finally approached Castle Maze and spied the dark green hedges of a giant maze ahead of him.

As he limped up to the entrance, he could see a group of people milling around.

"Heroes!" he muttered to himself. "Five third-class and two second-class."

"Are you here for the job, too?" a third-class hero asked Hal.

Hal nodded.

"We're waiting for a guide to take us through this maze," said another third-class hero, who was swishing his sword aimlessly from side to side.

Just then, a second-class hero wandered up. He was dressed in a yellow satin doublet and had on a purple sword belt with a long carved scimitar dangling from it. On his head he wore a black cavalier hat with white ostrich feathers. He made the third-class heroes, with their plain cotton tunics and knitted hose, look like servants.

"I don't know what you lot are waiting around for," he drawled. "The king will choose me over you any day. I've had far more experience. I don't expect you have even seen a sea monster, or a princess for that matter."

The third-class heroes shuffled their boots in the dust. It was quite true, none of them had ever seen a sea monster or a princess.

"If you're a second-class hero, where's your horse?" sneered a voice.

"Yeah!" said another. "Where's your horse?"

The second-class hero scowled. "I had to sell it," he said. "But I'm getting another one in a few days, after I finish this job."

The third-class heroes looked at one another and grinned. They knew what that meant. This hero, for all his fine clothes, was on his way down. He was broke. No hero sold his horse unless he was flat broke, and they instantly dismissed him as a threat.

All the same, thought Hal, I'd have sold my satin clothes before I sold my horse. He can't be much of a hero. He brushed past the satin-clad figure and entered the maze.

"You'll get lost if you go without a guide," a cheerful, round-faced hero called out to him. "You can be lost for days in there. They say that the place is full of tarondas!"

"Hundreds of people have been found dead in there," called out another voice.

"You'd better wait with us," advised a third.

Hal looked along the path in front of him. Tall dark green hedges grew straight up, shutting out the sun. He shivered. It smelt dank and musty, just the sort of place for tarondas. But he couldn't afford to wait. He had to be the first one to get to the king. So Hal took a deep breath and started along the path.

After about a hundred yards, the path turned a corner. Hal quickly took his sword out of its scabbard and looked carefully around him. Just the thought of tarondas made him feel ill. But of course he couldn't have let the heroes at the gate see that. He'd never seen a live taronda, but he'd seen the remains of someone a gang of tarondas had finished with! He swallowed hard and scanned the hedges again.

Just then, he came to the first fork in the maze. There was a path to the left and a path to the right. Which one should he take? What was it that the dwarf had told him?

Sweat broke out on Hal's forehead, and his heart began to thump heavily. He could not remember the dwarf's advice. Was it right or left, left or right? He wiped his face with the sleeve of his tunic and forced his mind to slow down and think back to the conversation with Rolf. Right was right. That was it. Seven right and then seven left.

Drawing a deep breath, Hal quickly took the right fork and counted it as one. He was worried that he would lose count and take the wrong turning so he plucked a small leaf from the hedge and held it in his right hand. If I pluck one leaf from the hedge every time I turn right, he thought, I can keep count, and when I have seven I will know to change directions.

So, plucking leaves at every fork, Hal counted seven right, then seven left, and seven right again. The maze seemed to go on forever, and Hal began to think that the dwarf was wrong. He was lost for sure, just like the poor souls he occasionally saw as he hurried along. Most of them were slumped down on the ground exhausted, a few were attempting to climb to the top of a hedge to try and see a way out, and one man had given up entirely and, with his cooking stove and small tent, had set up camp in the middle of the path. Hal had to step right over him as he passed.

Worse still were the bones. White dry skeletons, grinning up at him as he scurried by. Hal swallowed hard and wondered why he had ever thought being a hero was a good career. A teacher of giants or even a monster-tamer would have been a better choice.

And then, just as Hal had decided he was lost for sure, he turned a corner and there, in front of him, was a round green lawn. In the middle of the grass was a small ornamental pond with a fountain. He had found the middle of the maze.

Hal threw himself down on the cool grass with a great sigh, and cupped his hands to drink from the fountain. The fountain was in the shape of a giant snake surrounded by dozens and dozens of smaller snakes. The snakes were carved in grey and blue mottled marble and were so lifelike that Hal shivered as he stared at them. Hal didn't care for the design of the fountain at all. This King Maze had a weird sense of humor, he decided, as he knelt down and splashed water over his hot face and neck.

Then he thought of the dragon and opened up his leather bag and peered in. Two beady eyes blinked up at him. The dragon peeped lovingly, as it clambered out onto the marble rim of the pool and lapped at the water like a dog.

Hal noticed with dismay that the dragon was already growing bigger, and he could see the faint beginnings of the ridge-line forming down its spine. It was probably hungry again, too. Hal sighed. He had no food. It was as much as he could do to feed himself. How was he going to feed a growing dragon as well?

A strand of hair fell across his face and impatiently

he brushed it away from his eyes, but to his horror Hal found in his hand a writhing blue snake with scarlet eyes.

A taronda!

He flung it from him with a shudder, only to feel more snakes sliding round his neck and down his arms. He jerked around and saw to his amazement that the fountain had come to life with taronda snakes. Snakes were writhing and hissing and swarming around him. His arms were pinned to his sides and there were snakes wrapped around his legs and his neck. It had all happened so fast, he hadn't had time to struggle or reach for his sword.

The snakes around his neck tightened their grip and Hal began to choke and cough. Black spots danced in front of his eyes and his breath hurt in his throat. The last thing he noticed before everything went dark was that the dragon was making smoke.

Hal slowly opened his eyes. There was smoke everywhere and he couldn't see a thing. He put his hand to his neck. The last thing he remembered was the tarondas swarming over his body and squeezing him to death!

Suddenly, he was aware of a weight on his stomach, a weight that moved. The dragon squeaked in a terrified quaver and breathed another burst of smoke into the air.

Hal sat up gingerly. Well, what about that! It looked as though the dragon had saved his life. The tarondas must have been frightened off by the smoke. To make proper belching fire a dragon must be full grown, but even a hatchling dragon can make smoke. And if they get scared, that's what they do.

The dragon sidled up to Hal's face and began clacking its beak against his chin.

"Maybe you're not such a nuisance after all," said Hal, as he picked up the creature. "I shall have to give you a name as it seems I'm stuck with you." He thought for a moment. "I know. I'll call you Smoke, the Scourge of the Snakes. Smoke, for short."

Smoke, the Scourge of the Snakes dribbled a bit at this and tilted its head to one side. It was calming down and the smoke had given way to little puffs of breath.

Hal tucked the dragon into his bag, settled the bag on his shoulder, and, peering through the haze, looked for the path to take him through the other half of the maze. There were two exits from the center and he stood for a moment thinking. He must make sure he picked the correct one.

Six

THE AMAZE GAME

al thought for a while and tried to see the maze as a picture in his mind. He had just finished taking seven right turns, so surely now he should start on the left.

Holding his breath in case he was wrong, Hal turned left and walked briskly forward. Seven left, seven right, and then seven left. And before he had time to get anxious, out he came into the blazing afternoon sunshine. And there were the castle steps right in front of him.

At the top of the steps, two guards dressed in the red and orange livery of King Maze stared at his muddy clothes and crossed their halberds with a clash.

"I'm here for the job," Hal said quickly. "The rescue job. I'm a third-class hero. Am I in time?"

They didn't answer him, but stepped aside and allowed him to pass into the huge entry hall.

It was cool and dark inside after the sunshine, and Hal blinked as he tried to focus his eyes.

"King Maze will see you now," said a voice, and Hal whirled around to see a small dwarf in a red tunic looking up at him.

"If you'll come with me."

Hal followed him out of the hall and down a long corridor hung with tapestries. "Is your name Celti?" he asked, as he tried to shorten his long strides to match the small ones of the dwarf.

"Yes!" The dwarf stopped. "How do you know?"

"I met your cousin, Rolf," Hal said. "He told me to say hello and asked you to help me if you could." And he pulled the tiny wishbone from his tunic and handed it to the dwarf. "Hah!" said the dwarf. "The microbone! What a nerve that Rolf has."

"Microbone?"

"Haven't you heard of the microbird? I don't know, they don't seem to teach you anything at that Hero School nowadays. The microbird is, or I should say was, the smallest bird ever seen." The dwarf stopped and rubbed his stomach reflectively. "Delicious cooked in a spice pudding. We used to cook five hundred at a time. Extinct now, unfortunately. My family was very fond of microbird and we keep this bone as a sort of promise letter. Most of us can't write, you see." He rubbed the bone thoughtfully and put it into a leather pouch hanging from his belt.

"Promise letter?" said Hal.

"Yes. Now I have to promise to help you." The dwarf stared at Hal crossly. "What a nuisance." He pulled his long white beard. "Oh well. I'd better give you some advice. The king has already interviewed fourteen heroes for this job, but they have all failed to pass his test."

"What sort of test?" Hal said, alarmed. He hoped it was nothing too dangerous. Some of these kings had funny ideas about proving a hero's worth. He had heard some terrible tales about spiders and vampire bats.

The dwarf looked around to see if the passage was empty. "King Maze makes you play the Amaze Game," he whispered. "It's a game he invented. There's a tray with ten things on it. He lets you look at it for two minutes and then he covers it. You have to say what was on the tray."

"And none of the fourteen heroes managed it?" Hal said, surprised. "That's a standard test."

"No." said the dwarf. "Because there's a trick. Just remember, don't give him the names of the objects you see on the tray. You must give him names that rhyme with those objects."

"But why?" asked Hal. "That doesn't make sense."

"It does if you know that—" Celti stopped abruptly as a servant came towards them down the passage. "I can't say anymore," he whispered, and he hurried Hal along to the throne room.

King Maze was dressed in dark red robes, an orange cloak, and a heavy crown that seemed too big for his head. He had short legs that dangled without touching the floor and he drummed the back of his heels against the throne, impatiently.

"Hurry up. Hurry up!" he shouted. "Not got all day. Thirty more heroes being guided through the maze."

Hal scurried up to the throne and made a bow, almost tipping Smoke from the pack as he bent forward.

"Enough of that. Enough of that," scowled the king, putting up a hand to straighten his crown, which had slipped over one eye. "Look at this." He clapped his hands to a servant, who pulled a small table with a black cloth over it between Hal and the throne.

The king whipped off the cloth and there were the ten objects, as Celti had said. Hal quickly noted a carved jade fish, a round polished stone, and a diamond egg before the king said, "Two minutes to look. Two minutes. I cover them over again. You tell me what you saw. Understand? Understand?"

Hal nodded, a bit dazed by the king's habit of repeating words or leaving them out altogether.

"Good," said King Maze. "Begin."

Hal began to panic. He looked around for Celti, but the dwarf had disappeared. Should he obey the advice that Celti had given him?

Seven

A TERRIBLE MISTAKE

It was well known that dwarves were not to be trusted, but because of the microbone, Hal decided to take the risk and follow Celti's advice. When King Maze dropped his hand to show the time had begun, Hal stared at the tray, trying frantically to fix the ten objects in his head.

Besides the fish, the stone and the diamond egg there was a red pottery jug, a curl of blond hair (maybe from the head of the princess, thought Hal), a wooden handle, a fluted shell, a porcelain fox, a miniature tree in a silver pot, and a clay doll. Hal stared harder and harder. It wasn't difficult to remember the ten objects, but to find ten more objects that rhymed, that was very difficult.

"Right!" said King Maze, abruptly clapping his hands, and the servant immediately covered the table with the black cloth again. Hal, watching very closely, saw the servant press a small carved button at the side of the table.

"Right," continued the king. "What did you see? What did you see?" And he laughed and pushed his crown straight again.

Hal took a deep breath. He had to concentrate. The job depended on it.

"Er...I saw a dish...a bone...a peg, a mug, a pearl, a candle, a bell, a box, a bee..." Here Hal stopped. He could not think of a rhyme for the tenth object—the clay doll.

King Maze leaned forward, holding onto his crown with both hands. "Well?"

Hal puzzled hard. He was stuck. Beads of sweat broke out on his forehead.

"So," growled the king. "Failed, young man, you have failed."

"No!" Hal clenched his fists.

And then, as the king's words echoed in his ears, the solution came to him. The clay figure wasn't a doll at all. It was a carving of a man. And there was a good rhyme for that. "Fan!" he cried out. "A fan!"

King Maze gave a loud laugh and clapped his hands. The cloth was removed again, and the ten objects that Hal had named were on the table just as he had said. So, thought Hal, it was a trick table.

"Very clever. Very clever," said the king. "Fourteen

heroes tried, all failed." He looked Hal up and down. "You're nothing to look at. Never mind. Do you want the job?"

"Yes, please." Hal could hardly speak.

"Sign here," said the king, holding out a large parchment sheet. "This is the contract."

The servant brought a quill and ink stand and stood beside Hal. Hal picked up the quill and dipped it in the ink. He was so excited he could hardly write his name, and he was so excited that he forgot all the warnings that had been given in Hero School. Never sign a contract without reading it very carefully first. You never know what the fine print will say.

The servant blew some sand onto the manuscript to dry the ink, and then handed it to the king.

"Well, well," said King Maze. "Wish you luck. Yes, wish you luck. Find my daughter and you get to be my son-in-law. If you fail, ah well." The king waved his hand in dismissal. "Go see Celti. He'll tell you." And he pushed his crown straight and drummed his heels cheerfully against the throne.

Hal stumbled from the throne room, his thoughts churning. Son-in-law?

He saw Celti waiting in the passage and rushed up to him. "Celti, what did King Maze mean? Son-in-law?"

Celti shook his head and led Hal into a small room with a view of the sea from the window. "Dear me," he said. "I could see you didn't read that contract. Most unwise, if I may say so."

Hal caught hold of the dwarf's sleeve. "What have I signed?"

Celti frowned. "For one thing," he said, "you've agreed to marry the king's daughter. That is, if you manage to rescue her."

"Marry the king's daughter?" shrieked Hal. "But I don't even know her. How can I marry someone I don't know? Anyway, I don't want to get married for years yet. I want to have some fun first."

"Too late," said the dwarf. "You signed the contract, and that's not the worst anyway."

"Not the worst!" Hal gulped. "What else is there?"

"If you fail to get the princess...." The dwarf paused. "If you fail in the search, King Maze will have you hurled over the castle battlements into the sea."

Hal rushed to the window and leaned out. High above him rose the castle tower. He shuddered. It was a long way up. Then he looked down at the sea breaking on the rocks below, and shuddered again. It was an even longer way down.

The dwarf coughed and continued. "Let me tell you what happened. The Princess Lina, who is the king's only child, was out fishing last week when we saw a terrible sea serpent rise up out of the water and pick her up in its mouth. Then it swam off with her and she hasn't been seen since."

"Maybe she's dead," said Hal hopefully. "Maybe the serpent killed her."

"Ah," said the dwarf. "The Princess Lina is a clever princess. She managed to send a message back. A scallop shell washed up on the beach yesterday morning. Look!" He pulled a large pink shell out of his tunic. "Can you see some words? It's hard to read. Princess Lina has terrible handwriting."

Hal examined the shell closely. On the inside, there were some scratchings like chicken tracks. He held the shell up to the light to see better.

"They're hard to make out," he said. "But I think I see *Help* and *prisoner* and *eagles*."

"That's what I saw, too," agreed the dwarf.

"Well, help and prisoner are clear enough," said Hal. "But what about eagles?"

The dwarf shrugged. "You're the hero," he said. "I'll leave you to it. You can have a boat if you want. Everything in the castle is at your disposal."

Hal had a sudden thought. "But how will I recognize the princess? I don't know what she looks like."

Celti looked surprised. "Why, she looks like a princess, of course. She is dressed in a white princess dress with a golden princess girdle and matching tiara on her long hair. You will have no difficulty." The dwarf bowed formally and turned to go.

Hal nodded. "Fine," he said. "Er, do you think we could have some food?"

"We?" said the dwarf, surprised. "I thought there was only one of you."

Hal lifted his bag off his shoulder and pulled out the baby dragon. "Meet Smoke," he said.

The dwarf smacked his lips. "I haven't had dragon pie for a long time," he said. "If you like, I'll take it to the cook and—"

"You and your cousin," said Hal. "You know dragons are protected."

"Unfortunately," said Celti wistfully, and looked at Smoke with longing. "Ah, well. Help yourself to food in the kitchens. They're in the cellar." And he hurried out of the room.

Smoke nestled under Hal's chin and ooked at him.

"Come on," said Hal. "Let's get something to eat."

In the kitchens, there were great caverns of fires with cauldrons and spits, and dozens of servants rushing around busily. No one took any notice of Hal as he helped himself and Smoke to stew from a big pot on a fire, and then to ale from an oak barrel. They sat in a corner out of the way to eat, and then Smoke curled up in Hal's lap and burped happily.

"You weigh twice as much as yesterday," Hal told him. "I hope you're not going to keep this up."

A servant rushed past them with a plate of roast boar and nearly tripped over Hal's legs.

"Watch it!" he said.

"Now, when I'm a second-class hero, I'll get to eat in the dining hall instead of in the kitchen with the servants," Hal said to the dragon. "That's Rule #20. Second-class heroes are to be treated like gentry."

But Smoke wasn't listening. He was fast asleep. Hal sat there for a few moments, wondering how he was to start looking for the princess and trying not to think about what would happen if he did or did not find her, and then he, too, fell asleep.

The morning was just trickling in through the high window slits when Hal awoke, cold and stiff from the stone floor. He got up, and with the dragon tucked under his arm, he scrounged for some bread and cheese which he wrapped in a napkin. Then he found an empty bottle and filled it with water.

After getting lost in the miles of corridors, Hal finally found his way outside to the courtyard, where he saw Celti.

"Now," said Celti, "come this way." And he led Hal to a small postern gate set in the wall. "This gate will take you out onto the cliff path and down to the beach."

A black-bearded gatekeeper shambled sleepily up to them, unlocked the gate, and threw open the bolts.

"Thank you for all your help," Hal said to Celti as they shook hands. "I won't forget it."

"Don't mention it," said Celti. "Just promise me," he licked his lips, "if you ever want to get rid of the dragon, let me know first."

Hal shook his head. "You dwarves!"

The gate slammed behind him and he set off down the cliff path. Except for a few curious goats, which stopped their chewing to stare at him as he walked by, there was no one around. The cliffs and the beach were deserted.

Hal had decided that his first step was to get a boat and see for himself the spot where the princess had disappeared. There was a large rowboat on the beach and a small blue canoe. Hal chose the canoe and, putting his bag and the dragon in the bow, he pushed off from the rocky shore.

Eight

DANGER FROM THE DEEP

Hal paddled out to sea, and soon the walls of Castle Maze began to fade into the distance. This must be about where the princess was when she was carried off by the sea serpent, he thought. He paddled slowly around in circles, looking for something, a clue, anything, but only found driftwood and some floating beds of kelp. Maybe the princess had drowned after all. Maybe the people who saw the sea serpent were mistaken. But then he remembered the message on the scallop shell: *help, prisoner, eagles.*

The sun rose in the sky and the day grew warmer. Hal took Smoke and the bread out of his bag and, after breaking off a piece for the dragon, he ate the rest himself.

Smoke gulped the bread down fast and then perched on the rim of the boat with his curved talons, clucking with pleasure.

"You like sea travel, do you, Smoke?" said Hal conversationally.

The dragon flapped its wings to keep its balance.

Hal trailed his fingers in the water as the canoe rocked gently to and fro. "I'm getting quite fond of it myself," said Hal. "It seems a shame we have to try and find that princess." His fingers caught a tangle of seaweed. As he moved the fronds, a red round flower swam up to the surface.

"Look at the pretty sea flower, Smoke," Hal said, yawning. The sea air and the sunshine were making him sleepy.

The flower blinked twice and disappeared.

Hal swallowed hard, and dropped the seaweed. Not a flower!

Just then, there was a disturbance around the canoe and waves began to heave.

"Hold on, Smoke!" yelled Hal, as he grabbed the sides of the canoe.

The dragon's wings flapped helplessly, and it fell back onto the bottom of the canoe, its legs sticking up in the air. Then, with a rush of water that flipped the canoe over and flung Hal and Smoke into the sea, an enormous sea serpent reared its neck above the waves.

Hal froze with fear as he floundered in the water and gazed at the towering green neck of the monster, so long that it looked like the trunk of an enormous tree. And right at the top was a tiny head with two bulging horns and a pair of red glowing eyes like lamps, glaring down at him.

The dragon wailed pitifully as it struggled in the water, its claws and wings flailing to keep it afloat. Hal swam over to the dragon and it scrambled hastily onto his shoulders.

The sea serpent moved again with another rush of water, and its long neck began to swoop down towards them.

The dragon squeaked in terror.

Hal gulped and clung onto the side of the capsized canoe.

The red eyes of the sea serpent blazed down on Hal and Smoke, as it bent its head closer and closer to them. And then its mouth opened, and they could see the double row of savage teeth with their razor-sharp edges.

"Don't be hasty, Mr. Sea Serpent," Hal called out. "Don't do anything you'll regret." His hero etiquette teacher at Hero School had told him that in a tight situation politeness can help to deflect an enemy's rage. But the serpent had obviously never heard of this good advice.

"Hang on, Smoke," cried Hal. "He's coming for us now," and, taking a deep breath, he dived under the surface.

The dragon clung desperately to Hal's hair as he clawed his way downwards to get out of the reach of those terrible teeth. He stayed under until his lungs were bursting, and then, gasping for air, he shot to the surface.

For a moment, all Hal could do was suck in air frantically, but then, as he twisted around looking for the monster, he saw it was swimming away at top speed, a v-shaped wake spreading out behind it. Clutched in its jagged teeth was the blue canoe.

Hal felt despair creep over him. The water was ice cold and he knew he could not keep afloat much longer. As for Smoke, the dragon was so quiet and still that Hal feared it was dead.

And then, the wake of the sea serpent hit them, and a giant wave rushed them forward at tremendous speed. Hal couldn't breathe or hear or see. Smoke was ripped from him by the force of the water, and they were tossed about like pieces of driftwood.

Hal sat up slowly. He opened his eyes painfully and blinked. He was lying on a white sand beach. Behind him, the waves broke onto the shore, and ahead of him stood a ruined tower with ivy growing up the walls.

He got groggily to his feet and staggered a few steps, feeling bruised and battered all over. He looked around for the dragon, but couldn't see it anywhere. Maybe it had drowned, Hal thought. It was a wonder that he hadn't. He sat down on a rock and let the sun dry him. His bag was gone, too, with all the food and his Hero Handbook. It was against the rules to lose your Hero Handbook. Rule #102 he thought, but of course he could not check to make sure.

Next, he examined his sword. It was very wet and getting rusty. That was against the rules, too. And he sighed. None of his training had said anything about being shipwrecked, and he had the feeling that proper heroes didn't go in for that sort of thing.

There was a rustle in the sand behind him, and Hal whirled around, his sword outstretched.

"Come out from there!" he shouted at a hump moving in the soft sand. "Come out before I run you through!"

The hump wiggled slowly, and then an eye poked through and blinked. It was a round golden eye.

"Smoke!" Hal jumped off the rock, fell onto his knees, and started scrabbling at the sand. "Smoke!"

Smoke slowly emerged from the sand, sneezing and coughing.

"I thought you were drowned." Hal picked the dragon up and stroked it. "You must have been buried by that wave!"

The dragon coughed, rolled its eyes, sneezed, and then gave a giant burp.

"What have you been eating?" said Hal, suspiciously looking around.

Smoke, the Scourge of the Snakes sneezed and burped again.

And then Hal saw a scrap of paper stuck to the dragon's spine.

"That's a page from my Hero Handbook!" he shouted, as he plucked it from the dragon's back. "Smoke! You've eaten my Hero Handbook!"

Smoke blinked and coughed and then tried to sit on Hal's lap.

Hal pushed the dragon away. "Do you realize what you've done? What am I going to do without my handbook? And I just bet you ate the bag and all the food, too!"

Smoke crooned softly and tried to kiss him with its beak.

"Ouch!" Hal pushed the beak away. "Dragons shouldn't try to kiss people. They should save that for other dragons, and they should not eat Hero Handbooks and leather bags." But the dragon meant no harm and Hal found he could not stay mad at it for long. "Come on," he said. "Maybe there are people living nearby and we can beg some food."

Keeping the ruined tower at his back, Hal started walking along the sand, Smoke flopping along behind him, hiccupping softly.

There didn't seem to be any sort of habitation. And they had only walked for a few minutes when Hal saw the ruined tower in front of him, and realized he had walked in a complete circle. He was a castaway on an island.

"Well, that's it, Smoke," Hal said gloomily. "A deserted island. There must have been people here once because of that tower, but that could have been aeons ago."

Smoke hiccupped again and sat down on Hal's foot.

"Serves you right if you have indigestion," said Hal sternly, pulling his foot away.

There was not much else to explore except for the center of the island. Dispiritedly, Hal turned and followed a narrow path that wound its way inland.

Apart from a few pools of greenish water and some withered holly bushes, there was nothing to look at until they came to a sharp dip in the land. And there, sheltered from the winds, were three gnarled and knotted oak trees. And on the top of the oak trees were three great nests.

Nine

MYSTERY OF THE BIRDMEN

The nests, which were made of straw and twigs, were about twelve feet around. Hal stared at them with awe. He shaded his eyes with his hand and gazed upwards. They seemed to be empty.

Hal looked around cautiously and, although there was nothing in sight, he shivered a bit. The sun was beginning to set over the horizon and the sky was full of a red glow. Day was almost over. They needed somewhere to sleep. Just then, the sky became dark with black whirring shadows, and he saw three enormous eagles flying towards the island, their wings beating the air like cracking whips.

Hal grabbed Smoke and ran for cover. He raced breathlessly towards a small holly bush and, heedless of the prickles and the dragon's complaints, pushed his way into the middle of it and flattened himself against the ground. Maybe the eagles were friendly and maybe they weren't. But he was going to make sure first.

As the sun set across the sea, the great golden birds circled the nests three times, their beating wings causing small dust storms to whirl on the ground, and then, with screeching cries, they glided downwards to the nests.

The dragon didn't like the look of the eagles and started to squirm and squeak. Hal grabbed its beak and held it closed.

As he stared fixedly at the nests, Hal saw a rope ladder tossed over the side of each one. The ladders began to sway back and forth, and three young men appeared, dressed in tunics and leggings made of some sort of shimmering gold with coronets of gold on their heads. They were laughing and joking as they climbed swiftly down, and once on the ground they started stretching and exercising as though they had stiff limbs. Hal saw that one of the young men had something wrong with one of his arms. It wasn't an arm at all, it was a wing, an eagle's wing, and he had it tucked into his side.

Hal whistled to himself. This was powerful magic. He'd heard stories of how humans could be locked into the shape of an animal and only escape at sunset; and when dawn came, they were forced to take on the shape of the animal once more. He'd heard stories of such things, but he'd never believed them before.

The three eagle-men finished their exercising and then, single file, they walked down a narrow path until they were out of sight.

Hal crawled painfully out of the holly bush with the dragon. Something had just occurred to him. The princess had printed the word *eagles* on the scallop shell. *Help, prisoner, eagles.*

"What do you think, Smoke?" he asked. "Maybe I'm getting closer to the disappearing princess!"

Hal stared up at the nests. "I'm going to explore," he said. "You stay here and don't move." Putting the dragon down, he made a dash for the oak trees and swung himself onto one of the rope ladders.

It was a long way up to the giant nest lodged at the top of the tree, and the ladder swung wildly back and forth as Hal climbed doggedly upwards. It was enough to make you seasick, he thought, feeling green inside as he untangled his sword from the rungs.

Finally, Hal reached the nest, pulled himself over the top, and fell inside.

The first thing he noticed was the musty smell. It was so strong that he began to cough and sneeze. When he finally stopped and looked around, he noticed a small golden box at the bottom of the nest. It was elaborately carved, with rubies and sapphires decorating the lid. After a quick look over the side to check whether the eagle-men were coming back, Hal tried to open it. But the lid wouldn't move. He looked for a keyhole, but there didn't seem to be one. So he pulled and tugged at the lid again, but it remained obstinately shut.

There must be a magic spell that opens it, decided Hal, and he threw the box down in disappointment. To his surprise, the lid flew open with a snap.

Inside the box was a golden locket on a chain, and when Hal opened the locket he saw a picture of a young man with a coronet on his head and the words *Prince Carl of Aristo* written in silver around the rim.

Somewhere at the back of Hal's mind the name Aristo rang a bell, but he couldn't think why. He puzzled over this for a moment and then forgot it. This eagle-man had once been a prince, that was clear. But what had happened to change him into an eagle?

Just at that moment, there was a sudden commotion under the tree and Smoke's voice started wailing piteously.

Hal leaned over the side of the nest. The dragon was swaying from side to side in great alarm. What was the matter? And then he saw—the three eagle-men were coming back up the path.

Hal quickly ducked down out of sight, but it was too late. The eagle-men had seen him, and with a bellow of rage they raced towards the ladder.

Hal ran and looked over the side of the nest, but

the branches of the tree were too thin to bear his weight. There was nothing to do except draw his sword and prepare to fight.

The eagle-men swarmed over the edge of the nest and stood facing him.

"Churl!"

"Varlet!"

"Poltroon!"

Hal blinked. He wasn't sure what they were saying, but it didn't sound friendly.

"Who are you, varlet? How did you come here?" asked the one Hal recognized from the picture as Prince Carl.

Hal tried to smile pleasantly. They sure had a funny way of talking.

"Hi!" he said, swallowing hard. "I'm Hal, a third-class hero. I'm looking for a princess."

"As we are also!" said the eagle-man with the eagle wing. He looked younger than the other two, still a boy. "Alas. We are under a curse. We—"

"Silence, Petro," said Prince Carl sharply. "You talk too much."

"Yes. No more," said the third eagle-man angrily, snatching the box from Hal's hand. "Let us slay this churl and cast his body over the side."

Prince Carl nodded. "But first he will tell us his tale and how he came here," he said. "Speak, third-class hero."

Hal took a deep breath and, as the dark crept around them and the moon rose in the sky, he began to talk. He mostly told the truth, but there was one part he left out deliberately. He had just remembered where he had seen the word Aristo before.

Hal was a good storyteller and, before he had finished the three eagle-men were laughing and slapping their hands on their legs. When he came to the part about the princess and how she had been carried off by a sea serpent, the three eagle-men looked at one another and nodded knowingly.

"Have you got some news about the Princess Lina?" Hal asked quickly. He was sure from the way they had looked at one another that they knew something.

"Listen carefully, Hal, third-class hero," was the answer he got from Prince Carl. "You see before you the three princes of Aristo. I am Carl, the eldest. This," he nodded, "is Brian the younger, and this," he nodded again, "is Petro the youngest."

"Pleased to meet you," murmured Hal.

"Nearly sixteen years ago," went on Prince Carl, "we hunted in a forest near to our father's palace. It so happened that we slew the Prince of the Eagles with an arrow. When the King of the Eagles heard of this, he became enraged and sought revenge. He flew to our father's palace where he saw our baby sister, who was asleep in the garden. The King of the Eagles stole her away and she has never been seen since. Our mother, the queen, died of a broken heart, and our father blamed us for the tragedy. In his grief and anger, he cursed us to become eagles by day forever, or until we brought back his daughter to him. We have searched the country for our sister, but to no avail. We spend all our days searching for her, and as night falls we fly hither to our nests and turn back into our human form until the dawn."

There was a silence after he stopped speaking, and the three brothers wept.

Hal cleared his throat and wiped away a tear of his own. It was a very sad story.

"I may be able to help you," said Hal. "I think I know where your sister is. If I tell you, will you help me in return?"

The three brothers turned towards him with their eyes shining.

"If you can help us in our quest, we will grant you any boon you ask us," said Prince Carl.

"Does that mean yes?" asked Hal doubtfully.

Ten

PRISONER

"Is your sister's name Alta?"

"Yes! Yes!" the three brothers cried together.

"A girl who has a golden locket around her neck, just like the one in the box, lives on the seashore near Castle Maze. She doesn't know who she is."

The brothers buzzed with excitement. "Forsooth, it must be our sister," said Petro, "if she has the locket."

"Ah," said Prince Carl, with a sigh. "Maybe we shall be free once more."

"Now you must tell me about the Princess Lina," said Hal. "You gave me a promise."

"We will keep our promise," said Prince Carl. "If

you are right about our sister, we will fly back and tell you what we know about your princess."

"But if you are wrong about our sister, we will slay you," said Prince Brian grimly.

Hal thought this was highly unfair, but he didn't say so as it was three to one.

"Tell us some tales, hero," said Prince Petro. "It is a long wait for the day."

So, Hal told them all the stories he knew and, when he ran out of stories, he recited all the hero rules he could remember. It was rather boring, but the three princes didn't seem to mind. After sixteen years, they would have listened to anything.

Eventually dawn came: first a yellow line of light on the horizon, then a pink flush, and finally the sun itself broke over the edge and light flooded the sky.

The princes began to get ready for their change back into giant eagles. Prince Brian and Prince Petro climbed down the ladder and climbed up into their own nests.

"Why has Prince Petro got an eagle wing all the time?" Hal asked.

"I do not know," said Prince Carl. "But I think my father's curse began to fail as he got to Petro and that is the result."

Just then, Prince Brian called out from his nest, "Enchain the storyteller. If he is wrong and the maiden is not our sister, then we will cleave him in two when we come back."

Hal shivered. Did that mean what he thought it meant?

Prince Carl took a gold sash from around his waist and tied Hal's arms and legs. "There," he said. "You are our prisoner while we are gone."

"But you will come back!" Hal was alarmed.

"In faith, before dusk," smiled the prince. He gave a sudden screech, leaped into the air, and transformed into a golden eagle, flapping its giant wings and hovering above the nest. The other two eagles circled around, screeching for several minutes before soaring high up in the sky, where they became pinpricks of black against the sun. Then they disappeared.

After a while, Hal struggled to the edge of the nest and peered over. "Smoke?" he called. "Smoke?"

Hal called and called, but there was no answer from below. Finally, he sat down in the bottom of the nest to wait. When the eagle-men found their sister and the curse was lifted, they would fly back and release him.

Fly back? As he thought this, Hal's heart beat faster. How could they fly back? When the curse was lifted, they would be men! They would never fly again. He would be left in the nest to die!

Hal desperately pulled and tugged at his bonds, but the cord just dug even deeper into his arms and legs. Finally, he gave up and lay down in the bottom of the nest in despair.

He must have dozed off in the heat of the sun, for

when he heard the cry he jerked awake from a dream of a banquet where he was eating roast duck and rabbit pie.

He pulled himself to the edge of the nest and peered over.

There, right underneath the nest, was the dragon crying piteously.

"Smoke!" Hal shouted. "Where have you been?"

The dragon lifted up its head and carolled happily when it spotted Hal.

"I'm a prisoner up here," Hal called, and then he sighed bitterly and rolled back down into the nest. If only Smoke could understand.

As time went by, the dragon became more and more impatient. It cried and whined and rubbed itself against the tree.

The sun was making the inside of the nest like an oven, and Hal was despairingly rolling around trying to find a cooler spot, when he felt the nest begin to shake. Smoke was climbing up the ladder! Rung by rung the dragon clambered upwards, its wings flapping wildly to give it balance, and its teeth and talons gripping the rope. It got halfway up only to slip and fall back, screeching as it fell. But then it was up again, and finally its blunt grey head pushed over the top of the nest and the dragon fell inside with a rush of wings and a squawk of excitement.

"Smoke! What a clever dragon you are."

Smoke happily curled itself around Hal's neck and yawned.

"No! Don't go to sleep," Hal said quickly, and he waved his tied arms at the dragon. "Look! You must chew through these cords with your teeth!"

The dragon blinked its golden eyes at him.

Hal sighed. Then he put his head down and began chewing at the cords himself. "See," he said. "Chew! Chew!"

The dragon bent its head down and licked Hal's arms with its sandpaper tongue.

"No! Chew! Chew!" pleaded Hal desperately.

And then the dragon did. It opened its mouth and began chewing through the bonds with razor-sharp teeth.

Twang! The cords burst apart and Hal's arms were free!

"Smoke, you beauty!" said Hal, and he hugged the dragon. "Why did I ever say you were a nuisance? That's the second time you've saved me."

Smoke swallowed the braided cords with a satisfied gulp. Hal untied his legs and, after rubbing back the circulation, he tucked Smoke under his arm and slowly climbed down the rope ladder.

The dragon squirmed in Hal's arms and wriggled to the ground. Then it sniffed the air and started off down the path that the eagle-men had taken the night before. Every few feet it stopped and looked back anxiously, waiting for Hal to follow.

"All right, if that's what you think," said Hal. "Lead on." Although what it was that the dragon wanted him to see he had no idea.

They followed the path around a hump in a small hill and down towards the sea. A small stream chattered along beside them and Hal drank his fill from the clear water. Now, if only they could find some food, he thought, as his stomach rumbled.

The dragon hurried along the path ahead of Hal, and then disappeared. One moment it was there in the middle of the path, and the next it wasn't!

Hal ran forward. "Smoke?" he called. "Where are you?"

Eleven

THE TREASURE TRAP

There was an answering noise from somewhere under his feet, and then Hal saw a small hole by the side of the path, half hidden by a large boulder. He lay down and peered into the opening.

There seemed to be a narrow tunnel sloping downwards. This was obviously where the dragon had gone, for Hal could hear it somewhere at the bottom.

Hal wriggled his body into the hole and lowered himself cautiously down into the tunnel. It was dry and dusty, but the air seemed fresh, and there was a cool greenish light filtering up from the bottom. As he crawled along the rocky passage, his eye caught a flash of gold on the side of the tunnel, and he plucked a gold feather from where it had snagged on a sharp piece of rock. It was an eagle feather. Prince Petro must have passed this way.

All at once the tunnel levelled out, and he was walking upright towards a round hole carved in a solid rock wall. The green light was brighter, and there was a strong smell of seaweed and salt.

Hal clambered through the hole and found himself standing on a small rock platform, looking down on an enormous sea cave. Directly below him was a round pool of green water, lit by some kind of phosphorous light. At the edges of the pool were piles of boxes and barrels, great shining heaps of golden coins, small mountains of silver and pewter ornaments, jewelled swords, bales of silks and satins, kegs of glittering diamonds, and crates of smooth glowing pearls.

Hal whistled softly to himself.

A small voice murmured beside him. Smoke was staring down at the glittering piles with fierce concentration. Hal smiled. Dragons loved treasure. Even hatchling dragons, obviously. It must be in the blood.

He made his way carefully down the rock face to the floor of the cavern, with Smoke scrambling behind him.

It was very quiet and still. The only sound was the dripping of water on rock. Hal sniffed the air. Now he could smell a new scent. It was bitter, an acrid type of bitterness, a smell he had come across somewhere before.

The dragon called from behind him.

Hal turned to look, and burst out laughing. The dragon was jumping up and down and trying to bury itself in a pile of golden coins.

"Get out of there, you silly thing," he said, pulling the dragon out by its tail. "Come and help find some food, and don't make such a noise. The owner of this treasure must be somewhere around, and I don't expect he's friendly."

All around the pool, set back into the rock, were small dark caves. Hal ventured into a few of them. They seemed full of old rotting boxes, and smelt of decay and must. But when they had travelled about halfway around, they came across a cave that was brighter than the others. This cave was lit by a thin shaft of daylight, and inside Hal could see a very large glass bottle, and inside the bottle he could see something moving!

Hal pushed the dragon behind him and, drawing his sword, he approached the cave cautiously.

The glass bottle, which was almost as tall as he was, seemed to be full of a shifting, whirling shape. He crept closer and then stopped, his mouth open. The shifting, whirling shape had become the shape of a girl, a girl who was banging with her fists on the sides of the glass.

Hal ran forward quickly. "Help is on its way!" he called, waving his sword, as he jumped triumphantly forward.

The next thing he knew, he was dangling upside

down, his right foot caught in a snare. He had stumbled over a trip-wire.

"Oh, you stupid stupid boy!" cried a voice from the glass jar. "Just when I thought I was going to be rescued."

Hal swung to and fro on the wire, the blood rushing to his face.

"How was I to know there was a snare," he said crossly. "Do you think I did it on purpose?"

There was a sniff from the jar. "Who are you, anyway, and how did you get here?"

"I'm, Hal, a third-class hero, and I've been hired by King Maze to find the Princess Lina. Are you the Princess Lina?"

"Yes, of course I am," said the girl. "I might have known my father would be too mean to hire a first-class hero. Trust him to hire someone cheap."

Hal's face got redder. What a nasty girl. "I found you, didn't I?" he said.

"Well, of course you did. I sent a message, didn't I? I sent that scallop shell with the eagle-men."

"It wasn't much of a message that you sent," said Hal bitterly.

"Well, it got you here," said the princess crossly.

Hal thought about that. "No, not really," he said, and he started to struggle to get free of the wire.

"The eagle-men thought I was their sister," said Princess Lina. "They used to come and talk to me in the evenings before the serpent came back."

Hal twisted around on the wire. "Who put the snare here?" he asked.

"The serpent. He came back early yesterday and saw the eagle-men as they were leaving. The snare is for them."

"Is the serpent going to eat you?" said Hal, puffing nervously as he tried to untangle his sword, and thinking that the serpent would probably want him for dessert.

"No. I'm just a treasure. He likes to collect treasures. He's half dragon, you know. He collects anything that takes his fancy. He wrecks ships and does a bit of beachcombing. Anyway, he saw me fishing, and he decided to collect a princess."

"How did he know you were a princess?" asked Hal, still struggling with his sword.

"Oh, dragons and serpents always know. They can tell a true princess when they see one."

Hal swung around. "Can you tell if that's a true princess, Smoke?" he said to the dragon, who was sitting underneath him.

"What a dirty-looking creature. It hardly looks like a dragon."

"It's a hatchling," said Hal defensively. "And it's growing fast."

By now Hal had got his sword untangled and was trying to lift it up to the wire so he could cut it through.

"Do hurry up," said the princess. "If the serpent sees you, he'll kill you with one blast of his poisonous breath, and then I will have to stay here and wait for another hero. And I'm getting very bored of waiting."

"You don't care if I'm killed!" said Hal angrily. "You're just thinking of yourself!"

"Well, I am a princess, and you're only a third-class hero," she said in a reasonable tone.

Hal was so taken aback he couldn't speak. What a selfish, spoilt girl! He couldn't believe that this was a real princess—she was not at all like the princesses he had read about in Hero School. It would serve her right if he left her in the jar.

Hal managed to get the sword against the wire, and then, summoning all his strength, he strained his muscles and SNAP, the wire parted and he crashed to the ground. Smoke squeaked and scuttled out of the way just in time.

Hal had not cut the wire a minute too soon, for as he lay winded on the floor of the cave, there was a swishing and swirling of the water in the pool, and waves began to lap over the edge.

"Quick! Hurry!" yelled the princess, banging on the glass. "Get me out of here. The serpent is coming."

Twelve

THE CHASE

There was a terrible sucking noise in the water and a whirlpool started to spin round and round at a dizzy speed.

"He's coming!" yelled the princess again. "Do something, you stupid third-class hero!"

Poor Hal had had the breath knocked out of him by the fall. All he wanted to do was lie on the ground and breathe.

"Hurry up!" screamed the princess.

Hal staggered to his feet and gripped the glass jar with his arms. The only way he could think of to free the princess was to push it over. He just hoped it wouldn't break into pieces and cut her to bits.

"Hold on," he managed to say, and rocked the jar

backward and forward. Each time he rocked it, it swung farther, and then, finally, it teetered, swung in a circle, and fell on its side with a thud.

"Get out, then," shouted Hal to the princess, who was on her hands and knees in the jar.

"You useless hero," snapped the princess as she crawled out the neck of the bottle, adjusting her golden girdle and tiara. "A princess should be rescued properly."

Hal stared at her. She could at least say thank you. But there was no time to stand around. Already the tip of the serpent's head was bulging through the water, and then its glowing red eyes shot up, swivelled on their stalks, and saw them!

"Hurry!" Hal grabbed Smoke under one arm and the princess with the other. "We've got to get to the tunnel!"

There was a roar of rage and a giant wave broke over the edge of the pool and swept towards them as the serpent's green neck thrust upwards.

The princess stumbled, and Hal pulled her ahead of the wave and towards the hole in the cavern wall. But her long white dress caught on a nail sticking out of a barrel of silver.

"Oh, wait!" she cried. "My dress!"

"We can't wait," shouted Hal, and his sword flashed out and the long white dress became a short white dress. On they ran again, dodging around barrels and scrambling over piles of gold. Smoke was squealing, the princess was shouting, and Hal was breathless from pulling the princess and carrying the dragon, who was definitely bigger and heavier than ever.

The neck of the serpent seemed to fill the whole cavern like a giant snake as it writhed towards the fugitives. And the echoes from its roaring bounced off the rocks and filled every corner.

"He says that he wants me to come back," said the princess breathlessly. "He's sad to lose me. He says he won't hurt me, just you, he'll kill you."

"Will he now," said Hal, pushing her in front of him.

"Yes," she said. "Aoah! Aoah!" she called back.

"What did you say?" Hal said suspiciously.

"I just said goodbye. It's only polite. A princess is supposed to be polite at all times."

Hal shook his head.

Just then, they came to the hole in the rock.

"Quickly, through the hole," urged Hal, "and up the tunnel." He glanced back hurriedly. The red stalk eyes and the great grinding, snapping teeth were almost upon them.

The dragon scuttled ahead up the tunnel, followed by the princess and Hal. But the head and neck of the serpent were through the hole in the rock and writhing after them.

"Hurry!" shouted Hal. "He's almost got us!"

Then the serpent opened its mouth wider, letting forth a blast of poisonous breath, and the green cloud shot up the tunnel. Hal started to cough and choke.

The princess looked back and screamed as she saw the cloud drifting towards her. "Don't breathe!" she cried. "Hold your breath!"

The cloud whirled around them as they stumbled upwards. Hal's head felt as if it would burst, and there was a pounding in his ears like hammers and drums. Through the haze, he saw a flash of daylight and knew they were nearly at the entrance. But could he make it? He could hardly move his limbs. His legs were so heavy...so...heavy. It was no use. Hal lay down on the rock and his eyes closed.

Cold water hit Hal in the face. He shuddered and opened his eyes. As he stared at Princess Lina in a dazed way, she filled her shoe with water and, *splash*, she threw it on him.

Hal coughed and spluttered. His head was pounding and his throat felt as if it were on fire. "Water!" he croaked. "Water!" The princess shrugged, and threw another shoeful over him.

"No...to drink!" Hal spluttered.

"Oh!" The princess handed him the shoe filled with water, and Hal drank. A shoe seemed a strange thing to drink from, but he was in no shape to argue.

"Where are we?" he asked. "What happened?"

"We're outside that awful tunnel. I had to pull you out. I saved your life and now I'm letting you drink from my shoe," said the princess grandly. "You are very lucky."

"Am I?" said Hal, who was beginning to recover.

"Yes, you are," said the princess. She seated herself by the bubbling stream and tried to wash some of the dirt from the tunnel off her arms and legs. "If I hadn't dragged you out, you would have died from the serpent breath. But you can thank me later."

Hal stared at her.

A voice crooned next to him and Smoke rubbed gently against him.

"Oh, Smoke!" said Hal. "You're all right!" And he scratched the dragon behind its ears.

"Well!" said the princess. "What now, third-class hero, Hal? How are you going to get me back home?"

Hal looked around helplessly. "I don't know," he said. "This is an island and I don't have a boat."

"You're not much of a hero, are you? If you haven't got a boat, you must make one."

"Make one?" said Hal. "I've never made a boat. They don't teach you things like that at Hero School."

"Well, they should," said the princess crossly.

Hal got to his feet and picked up Smoke. "Let's go and see what we can find."

Princess Lina sniffed. But she followed them down the path towards the sea.

The tide was out and the sand was white and hot. They wandered up and down the beach. The dragon found some small fish in a rock pool, scooped them up with its claws and ate them. Hal was very envious. He was so hungry that his stomach was gnawing like an animal inside him.

But then Princess Lina surprised him.

"Lend me your sword," she said, bending over a pool of water.

"Why?" Hal said. "Rule #2. I'm not supposed to lend my sword to anyone."

"Fiddlesticks!" snapped the princess. "You want to eat, don't you?"

"Yes," said Hal.

"Well, then."

The thought of food was so tempting that Hal meekly handed over his sword, hilt first.

The princess turned to the baby dragon and spoke slowly. "Oaok...koaao...ooh!"

Smoke looked at her enquiringly for a moment, and then bounded to the pool of water and scooped out four small fish onto the rocks, where they flopped and squirmed in the sunlight. The princess sliced each one neatly with the sword and then cleaned it.

Hal was horrified at his sword being used in this way. First toasting cheese and now cleaning fish. It would all be recorded on the memory jewel. He would be laughed at by everyone.

"Did you speak to Smoke in dragon language?" he asked finally.

She nodded. "I had a tutor who taught it to me. It's too bad they didn't teach you anything useful at that school. Dragon is a very useful language."

"Only if you have a dragon," protested Hal. "And how many people have dragons nowadays? Not very many. I'm probably the only hero with a dragon. We learned giant language."

"Giant!" laughed the princess, who was now sitting down with two sticks and rubbing them together over a pile of dried seaweed that she had arranged on top of a large reddish rock. "Giant! But most giants speak our language now. What's the use of speaking giant?"

"All heroes should speak giant," said Hal defensively.

Princess Lina rubbed the sticks harder. "I was taught the common tongue," she said. "So I could talk to the servants and common people, like you."

"Oh," said Hal stiffly. "I don't think heroes are common people."

The princess didn't answer. She was too busy blowing on the small spark that she had made. Then the spark grew to a flame and the flame licked at the dry seaweed. Carefully, she fed small twigs and sticks to the blaze and soon had a roaring fire. She skewered the four fish on Hal's sword and held them over the heat.

But then she screamed "Ahhh!" and dropped the sword. She held her fingers up to her mouth. "I've burnt myself!"

"Heat travels through metal," said Hal. "You have to wrap something around the handle."

The princess muttered under her breath and tore a strip of material from her skirt and wrapped it around the hilt like a bandage.

"That's better," she said. "How did you know that?"

Hal gave her a superior smile. "Oh, I just know these things," he said. "When you're a hero, you have to know things like that."

When the fish were cooked, Hal and the princess ate every morsel. Then they sucked the bones.

"How did you learn to do all this?" asked Hal, waving his arms at the fire and the fish bones.

"Princess Camp," said Princess Lina, licking her fingers. "Every summer, my father sends me to Princess Camp. They teach you how to be a proper princess and give you helpful hints about being kidnapped and imprisoned. They taught us karate, and survival skills. But," she chewed at a bone thoughtfully, "karate isn't much use against a sea serpent."

"Did they teach you how to build a boat?" asked Hal hopefully.

Princess Lina shook her head. "It's against the rules to rescue ourselves. Survival is all right, but not rescue. Princesses are supposed to be rescued by someone else."

"That's crazy!" said Hal.

"No crazier than a lot of your hero rules. If princesses rescued themselves, a lot of heroes would be out of a job."

Hal had never thought about that. It was a good point. "If you're a princess, you're brought up to try and help common people, not to put them out of work. It's a real nuisance, but there it is. Of course," she went on sensibly, "if no one had come I would have rescued myself. I'm not crazy."

Hal did not like to be referred to as a common person, and said so.

"Sorry," said the princess unrepentantly. "Now, let's get on with getting off this island."

But Hal wasn't listening. He was staring at the fire. It seemed as though the fire was moving. It *was* moving. The red rock the princess had built the fire on was moving upwards, and the fire scattered violently in all directions.

Thirteen

A DEADLY RIDDLE

Smoke hid behind Hal, who drew his sword and waved it in the air. There was a rumbling like thunder and the ground shook under them. Boulders began to roll along the beach and waves slapped against the shore. The reddish rock moved sideways.

"It's a toe, a giant toe!" shouted Princess Lina, and she grabbed hold of Hal's tunic. "There's another one, and—"

"A whole foot!" Hal's voice trembled. "And if there's a foot—"

"There has to be a leg, and a body!" Princess Lina gulped.

"Let's get out of here!" Hal grabbed Smoke and

backed away. "We've just lit a fire on the toe of a sleeping giant!"

Too late.

There was a rush of wind around them and suddenly they were flying through the air on the giant palm of a giant giant.

"Do something!" Princess Lina squeaked, as they were rushed upwards. "You're supposed to be a hero—and didn't you say you spoke giant? Talk to him!"

"Talk to him!"

"Yes. Say something, or else he's going to eat us!" Her voice ended on a very unprincess-like squeak as they arrived level with the giant's face.

Hal swallowed hard. He had to force his eyes to keep open. The sight of the giant's face at such a close distance was fearsome. His eyes were two black lakes fringed with lashes like tree trunks. And as for his mouth! It was a great cavern circled with red, and inside the cavern were rows of jagged white mountain peaks.

"Ah! Oh!" roared the giant. "Who's been ticklin' me toe?"

The wind from the giant's breath knocked Hal and the princess flat, and if the giant's palm hadn't been cupped, they would have been blown off.

"Get it? Get it?" The giant laughed a thunder clap of laughter. "Ah, oh—ticklin' me toe!" and he laughed again at his own rhyming wit.

"Garlic!" Princess Lina held her nose as she scrambled to her feet.

Hal waved his sword and thought about jabbing it into the giant's thumb, but decided that the giant would hardly feel a pinprick, and put the sword away again. How did a hero fight a giant? He tried desperately to remember what he had been taught at Hero School. Giants were not generally supposed to be very bright, he remembered that. And they were big, but that was obvious. And they were always fighting one another. But none of this information was very helpful.

"Talk giant to him." Princess Lina tugged at Hal's arm. "Go on. Try and get him friendly."

Hal cleared his throat. "Er...Mr. Giant..." He cleared his throat again, nervously. His voice seemed to want to stick in the back of his stomach. "Yilhini, yolhim...yeye?" he shouted.

"Huh! What sort of stoopid talk is that?" roared the giant. "Can't you talk proper?"

"I was talking to you in giant," shouted Hal.

"That were giant?" The giant puffed up his cheeks, and laughed and spluttered, and slapped his free hand on his thigh. Hal, the princess, and Smoke rolled helplessly as they were whipped around with the giant's mirth.

"I thought that were a bird twittering!" the giant boomed.

"So much for your giant skills!" Princess Lina snapped at Hal. "What sort of giant taught you anyway?"

"It wasn't a giant," Hal said with a shrug. "It was a hero teacher who had learned it from a book."

"I might have guessed as much."

"It made the giant laugh," said Hal. "Look on the bright side."

Princess Lina frowned. "I'll talk to him," she said. "He'll listen to a princess." She tossed back her hair and stood as tall as she could. "I would like you to know, giant," she said, "I am a princess. I am the Princess Lina. And if you hurt me my father, King Maze, will kill you."

"Huh! What's that you says?" the giant boomed. "Don't whisper, girl. I ain't hearing you so good. Speak up proper."

Princess Lina opened her mouth as far as it would go, and shouted her speech again.

"Lina, eh! Purty name." The giant nodded his head and pushed clouds around the sky. "But I says all that princess stuff is downright stoopid. Lot o' stoopid nonsense."

"A lot of nonsense!" Princess Lina spluttered. "How dare—"

"Don't argue with him!" Hal hissed. "We have to keep him friendly. What does it matter what he calls you?"

"What does it matter!" the princess hissed back. "Of course it matters. Has he no respect?"

Hal sighed, and then, cupping his hand around his mouth, he shouted upwards. "My name is Hal, Mr. Giant. I'm a third-class hero and this is my dragon, Smoke." He pointed at the dragon, who was trying to hide behind the princess.

83

"Hi there, Hal. Hi there, Smoke," boomed the giant cheerfully. "I'm right pleased to meet youse. Youse can call me Basil. Everyone calls me Basil the Bore. I ain't sure why, though."

And with these words, the giant cupped his fingers over them and whirled his arm around a few times.

"Fun, huh?" he said, as he opened up his hand again and watched the three prisoners, who were now upside down and trying desperately to get back their balance.

"Oh, lots of fun," shouted Hal, his breath coming in gasps.

"What about this?" chuckled the giant genially, and he tossed them up into the air. Smoke wailed as they soared upwards and then plummetted down, the wind rushing and eddying around their bodies.

"Gotcha!" laughed the giant, as he snatched them in mid flight.

"Lotta fun, eh, Lina?" He laughed again.

"Why...you..." she gasped, as she fell backwards and tried to get her breath. "This giant is the most disrespectful—"

"Yes, yes," said Hal, as he turned himself right way up. He was getting tired of the Princess Lina's complaints. She was not at all the way he thought a princess should be. He gave himself a shake. What a terrible thing for a third-class hero to be thinking. If only he hadn't lost his Hero Handbook. A hero needed a handbook at a time like this.

"Hey, Mr. Giant!" he called, as loud and friendly as could be. "You seem like a good sort of giant. How about helping us off this island."

"You want I should throw youse?" bellowed the giant, his cavernous mouth stretching into a grin a mile wide.

"No! No!" Hal shouted back. "No, we don't want to be thrown. I was thinking more about being carried. It would only take you a couple of steps to cross the sea."

The giant gave a belly laugh that knocked them all around again.

"I got an idea," he roared. "Youse play the riddle game with me. If youse win, I gives youse a free ride."

"What's the riddle game?" Princess Lina asked Hal.

"It's an old-fashioned sort of test," said Hal. "You ask each other riddles, taking turns. The first one to answer wrong loses. I was told about it in hero history, but no one plays it anymore."

"Well, this giant wants to. But what I want to know is, what happens if we lose."

She raised her voice. "What happens if we lose?"

"I eats youse," boomed the giant happily.

"Oh," said the princess.

"What do you think?" said Hal. "Shall we play?"

"I guess we have to play." The princess made a face. "I just hope that school taught you some good riddles. It didn't seem to teach you anything else."

"Giants aren't too bright," said Hal hopefully, ignoring her remark.

"I goes first. I asks the first riddle." The giant laughed heartily, and then chanted in a slow deliberate voice:

"Which weighs more
When all's been said,
A pound of feathers
Or a pound of lead?"

The giant gave a giant grin. "Yous'll never get that," he said. "I could really eat youse now."

But Hal just grinned back. "That's an old one," he said, bellowing loudly. "The answer is, they both weigh the same."

The giant grunted and his grin shrank. "Huh!" he growled. "Thinks youse clever, don't ya!"

"Now answer ours," shouted Hal, who had been desperately trying to remember a riddle without any success. "Quick!" he said to the princess. "Think of a riddle."

"I'm trying," she said. "But I can only remember one."

"Well, ask it, ask it!"

The princess cleared her throat. "Here you are, giant," she shouted. "Guess this one:

"Riddle me, riddle me,
What is that?

Over the head
And under the hat?"

Hal groaned as the giant started chuckling with glee.

"Hair! Hair!" said the giant triumphantly.

"Everyone knows that one!" Hal snapped. "Couldn't you think of something better than that?"

"At least I thought of something," said the princess. "Which is more than you could do...hero."

"Now," said the giant. "Here's my second one. Youse'll never get this:

"Purple, yellow, red, and green.
A king cannot reach it, nor yet a queen.
Nor can a giant, whose height is so great.
Tell me this riddle while I count to eight."

The giant then started to count slowly. "One. Two. Three."

"What has a lot of colors?" Hal puzzled.

"Something that's very high up," said the princess. "Something no one can reach..."

"Five...six..." tolled the giant gleefully, licking his lips. "Seven..."

"It's a rainbow!" shouted Hal.

The giant roared and kicked the ground so hard that poor Smoke, who had been curled up having a nap, was rolled around and around like a ball.

"We have another chance. Let's think of something better." Princess Lina's forehead wrinkled in thought.

There was silence, except for the giant's heavy breathing.

"I've got another one." Princess Lina clicked her fingers. "Hey, listen to this, Basil the Boring."

"Wait—" said Hal.

But the princess took no notice.

"Riddle me ade. Riddle me ode.
Why did the chicken
Cross the road?"

"NO!" Hal stared at her in horror. If there was any riddle that the whole world knew, it was that one. He opened and closed his mouth like a goldfish. They were absolutely done for. If he had some salt and pepper, he would season himself and lie down.

"Goodbye, Smoke" he said, and patted the dragon fondly on its spiny head.

"Goodbye, princess," he said. "It's been a..." He was going to say, "it's been a pleasure to meet you," but since it hadn't, he stopped. He thought of saying, "it's been an interesting experience," but decided that being eaten, although an experience, would probably not be interesting.

"What do you mean, goodbye?" Princess Lina said. "He's never going to guess that riddle. I only heard it myself last summer at Princess Camp."

"Princess Camp!" Hal squeaked sarcastically. "That Princess Camp really leads the way in fashion!" He sat down on the giant's palm and put his hands over his ears and closed his eyes.

"What do you mean?" Princess Lina said crossly. "Look at him. He can't get it. I told you. It's a good riddle."

Hal opened his eyes and stared up at the giant. He didn't believe it. But she was right. The giant was blinking and winking and rolling his eyes round and round as if to help him think.

"Do you give up?" shouted the princess.

"No!" roared the giant.

There was a long silence.

"The chicken crossed the road...to eat its dinner," the giant barked.

"No."

"To lay an egg."

"No."

The giant scratched his head with a free finger.

"Last chance," sang out the princess.

"To go to sleep."

"No!" Princess Lina clapped her hands. "You've lost, Basil the Bore. You've lost. The chicken crossed the road to get to the other side!"

There was a long silence as the giant thought about this. "Huh! That's stoopid," he said finally. "That's a very stoopid riddle."

"You're just saying that because you didn't know the answer," said the princess.

Privately, Hal agreed with the giant, but of course he didn't say so. He was absolutely amazed that the giant hadn't known the answer.

"But it's not fair," the giant sulked. "I wants another chance."

"No. Absolutely not." Princess Lina pointed her finger at him. "Now stop whining. You have to keep your word and get us off this island."

"Oh, do I," said the giant.

"Right now," ordered the princess. "And hurry up about it." Hal wished she wouldn't be so bossy. He had a feeling that the giant didn't appreciate it.

And he was right.

The giant smiled a nasty smile. "Youse wants me to get you off this island?" he said.

"That's what I keep telling you," shouted the princess. "Really, you are slow-witted."

"Slow, am I," said the giant. "We'll see if I'm slow." And with that, he closed his fingers around the prisoners and, winding up his arm, tossed them out to sea.

"Youse are off the island now," he laughed. And he strode off across the water muttering, "Slow, am I? Huh."

Hal, Princess Lina, and Smoke hit the water with a splash and slowly started to swim back to the island. The dragon wailed and paddled frantically, spraying water everywhere, until Hal and Princess Lina managed to tow it between them. It was a long cold swim.

Fourteen

ESCAPE

They splashed their way to the shore in silence, and flopped down on the sand, cold, out of breath, and out of temper.

"Well, third-class hero," said Princess Lina, as she wrung out her hair. "You're not doing so well, are you."

"Me!" said Hal, astonished. "Who was it that annoyed the giant so much that he threw us into the sea?"

"I just told him to hurry up."

"You told him he was slow. Giants don't like that."

"It was true." Princess Lina said crossly. "Just think of the way he talked. He obviously never went to school."

"Yes," said Hal, getting impatient. "But just because it's true doesn't mean you had to make him angry. If you weren't a princess...I'd..."

Princess Lina jumped to her feet and flexed her arms. "If you want a fight, I'll fight," she said. "But remember, I've taken karate for three years, and not just from someone who's read about it in a book."

Hal groaned. That was all he needed, to be beaten up by the princess he was supposed to be rescuing. That would look good back at Hero School.

"Look," he said. "This is getting us nowhere. Let's try and think of a way off this island. Let's try and—" He stopped and ducked hurriedly, as the dragon, who had been snoozing under a blanket of sand, suddenly stood up on its hind legs and flapped its wings in large circles, causing a small sandstorm.

"Stop that, Smoke!" shouted Hal, brushing the sand out of his hair.

"Ugh!" spat the princess.

The dragon belched loudly and tried to put its head onto Hal's shoulder. But it had grown too big and tumbled Hal onto the ground.

"Smoke! Cut it out!" Hal staggered to his feet. "You're getting too fat." All that fish must have had a dramatic effect. Its stomach looked like a basketball.

Princess Lina looked at Smoke critically. "Do you think it can fly yet?" she asked. "Do you think it could take a message off the island?"

"That's an idea." Hal stared at the dragon too, and Smoke stared lovingly back at him with golden eyes.

The dragon certainly looked more like a proper dragon. Its scales were changing from a dirty grey to a reddish orange with flecks of scarlet and gold. Its back ridge was pointed in sharp v's and its tail was now five times as long as it had been when Hal had found the hatchling. And, as Hal stared, he noticed tiny smoke rings floating up from the dragon's nostrils. But could it fly?

"Get up, Smoke," Hal urged the dragon. "And let's see those wings."

The dragon thumped its tail on the sand, but didn't move.

"Look, Smoke, look!" Hal flapped his arms up and down wildly. "Do this!"

"Do you have any idea how silly you look?" Princess Lina said scornfully.

"Instead of being sarcastic, you might help!" Hal turned to her. "Get up and flap your arms, too. Or don't you ever want to get off this island?"

"I want to be rescued," said the princess. "I don't want to make a fool of myself jumping around and waving my arms." And she turned to the dragon. "Aoa ooa," she said. "Fly."

Smoke looked at her and rolled over.

Princess Lina shrugged, and soon both Hal and the princess were running around and jumping off rocks with their arms waving up and down.

The dragon watched them curiously, its head tilted to one side.

"Come on, Smoke. Come and join the fun," called Hal. "Show us how you can fly."

The dragon lumbered to its feet and began running towards Hal, whistling cheerfully.

"Up here!" called Hal, jumping onto a large rock and scrambling to the top. The dragon followed him and stood swaying, the breeze rattling its neck scales.

Hal flapped his arms up and down furiously, and jumped. It was at least a ten foot drop, and he landed with a shock and bruised his elbow on his knee.

"This had better be worth it," he muttered.

Smoke hesitated on the edge, looking down at Hal in a worried fashion.

"Jump, Smoke!" Hal encouraged him.

"Jump, Smoke!" shouted Princess Lina.

The dragon looked down again and then opened up its wings and flapped them furiously. A gust of wind caught them and it sailed off the rock into the air!

The dragon cried out in a terrified wail, flapped its wings in fear, and suddenly soared way up into the sky. It became a speck against the sun.

Princess Lina clapped her hands. "Oh, well done!" she called. "Doesn't it look beautiful?"

Hal nodded. He had a lump in his throat. It was a great sight to see a dragon fly, especially when the dragon belonged to you.

"Where has it gone?" The princess shaded her hand against her eyes. "It's gone so high I can't see it at all."

But just as she said this, a point of black came hurtling towards them. It was the dragon, falling, with wings clamped close against its body.

"You'll crash!" Hal cried. "Use your wings, Smoke! Use your wings!" And he flapped his arms up and down in encouragement.

Princess Lina hid her head as the dragon's shadow grew larger and larger.

"Fly, Smoke! Fly!" Hal screamed.

And then, just before the dragon crashed onto the ground, it stuck out its wings like brakes and did a sort of belly-flop landing into a thick prickle bush.

Hal and the princess raced over and pulled it out. Smoke croaked pathetically. Hal sighed and began pulling out the thorns that had stuck into the dragon's scales.

"I guess Smoke is going to need a lot of practice." Princess Lina shivered and looked up at the sun, which was sinking into the sea. "It'll have to wait until tomorrow," she said. "It will be night soon and we have to find somewhere to sleep. And," she added, holding out her palm, "it's also starting to rain."

The only shelter on the island was the ruined tower and they huddled under the broken-down walls, with the warmth of Smoke their only blanket. The rain cascaded down and a cold wind whipped through the cracks and holes.

Hal drew his sword and prepared to keep watch. He seemed to remember from the Hero

Handbook that heroes should stay on guard when rescuing princesses. But he had forgotton what number the rule was. And as he searched his mind trying to remember, he fell into an uneasy sleep.

"Atshoo! Atshoo!"

They were awakened at dawn by great sneezes that sounded like explosions.

"Smoke's caught a cold," said Hal anxiously, looking into the dragon's red and weepy eyes. "I didn't know that dragons could catch cold. What can we do about it?"

"Never mind that right now," said the princess, shivering. "If we don't get off this island, we'll get something worse than colds. The rain's stopped and the wind is dying down. Let's get moving."

Outside the ruined tower, it was a grey overcast day.

Princess Lina shivered again. "All right, hero," she said sulkily. "What do you suggest?"

"We can't wait for Smoke to learn to fly," said Hal. "I guess we'll just have to try and make a raft. If we cut down some trees and tie them together with some rope, that should do it."

"But how do we cut trees down?" said the Princess, trying to comb some of the tangles out of her hair with her fingers.

Hal sighed. "With my sword, I guess." And he patted his scabbard sorrowfully. What a comedown for a hero sword. Toasting cheese, cleaning fish, and now chopping down trees!

They walked along the beach until they found a stand of thin saplings, and Hal drew his sword and began cutting through the trunks. Smoke went to sleep and the princess started to look for something that could be used to bind the trunks together.

"Nothing," she said wearily, after she had gone right around the island.

"What about the rope ladders from the eagles' nests?" said Hal, looking up from trimming his tenth trunk.

"All gone," said the princess sadly. "They must have blown away in the wind last night. The nests are in pieces and the ladders have vanished."

"There must be something we can use." Hal looked at his blunt sword and sighed.

"There is," said the princess. "I was hoping it wouldn't come to this, but we haven't any other choice. You'll have to cut my hair off."

Hal stared at her long tangled golden hair. "How will that help?" he said.

"I can braid it into a rope," said the princess. "It's very strong."

"If you say so," said Hal doubtfully, and he picked up his sword and grabbed her hair.

"Ouch!"

"Keep still, if you don't want your throat cut. It was your idea."

"That's all the thanks I get," said the princess angrily. "Here I am giving up my precious hair to help make a raft that will probably drown us."

"If you don't want to be rescued, say so," said Hal. "We can stay on this island for the rest of our lives." His stomach growled hungrily.

"All right. All right." Princess Lina grabbed the handfuls of hair falling from her head and started to braid them into a long rope.

She certainly looked odd with her shorn spiky hair, thought Hal, as he put away his nicked and blunted sword. Not at all the way a princess was supposed to look. But he decided not to say anything. He wasn't too sure that he looked like a hero anymore either.

The raft, when finished, was not an elegant craft. It consisted of ten crooked tree trunks tied together with the hair rope, the princess's girdle, and a few strips from Hal's tunic. But it did float. It listed to one side, but, as Hal said, as long as Smoke sat on the other side, they were all right. He cut some branches for paddles, and Princess Lina filled some shells she had found with water from the spring.

Between them, they pulled a very reluctant dragon on board. It was too big to fit properly and its tail had to hang into the sea.

"We can use Smoke's tail as a rudder," said Hal, and he pushed off from the shore.

They paddled hard until the island was faint in the distance.

"I hope we're going in the right direction," said Princess Lina, breathing hard. "Do you know the right direction?"

Hal nodded. In fact, he didn't have a clue, but since she didn't either, it made no difference which way they went. It was all luck.

"Maybe we'll see a ship," he said.

"As long as we don't meet the sea serpent," said the princess gloomily.

Hal had forgotten about the sea serpent and wished that the princess had not reminded him. He felt uneasy thinking that the monster might be underneath them at that very moment, just waiting to surface and toss the raft to pieces.

Dark came and found them with blisters on their hands, ravenously hungry, tired, and irritable. They tried to sleep a little, but it was hard to sleep with water constantly washing over the side and soaking them. Even the dragon, who could sleep most places, grumbled and groaned until Hal poked it with a paddle and told it to shut up.

Hal was dozing fitfully, his mind full of half-dreams of roast chicken and plum pie, when a terrible noise exploded under the raft. BOOM! BOOM! The raft tossed and heaved in all directions. Hal was thrown to the edge and rolled helplessly toward the sea.

Fifteen

THE MONSTER

Waves burst into Hal's face. He grabbed for a piece of wood and clung to it. He could hear Smoke's cries of fear and the princess shouting, "Hal! Help! Help!"

Princess Lina was in the sea, splashing furiously and trying to pull herself back on the raft.

Hal wriggled over to her and grabbed her wrist. "Hang on!" he yelled. "Don't let go."

The princess pulled on his hand and heaved herself slowly out of the water. "Ah!" She shivered.

BOOM! BOOM! The raft heaved again, and as Hal, the princess, and Smoke clung to the wood, an enormous silver crab, with pincers the size of houses, rose out of the sea.

Hal stared in astonishment as the crab reared upwards, its pincers waving in the air, opening and shutting with the noise of thunder.

BOOM! BOOM! A shadow fell over the raft as the giant crab hovered ever closer.

"What are you going to do?" The princess gripped Hal's arm. "This monster is going to crush us!"

Hal watched the clumsy jerking movements. He had an idea. "There's just one chance," he said.

The pincers of the monster crab came nearer and nearer, jerk by jerk, opening and shutting with booming crashes like the sound of drums.

Hal unsheathed his sword and swiftly cut the rope that bound the tree trunks together. He pulled up one of the logs and then, just as the claw hovered above his head, he hurled the log, like a javelin, right up into an open pincer.

The monster crab stopped abruptly. Its claws seemed to seize up and it lurched sideways. Then, with a tremendous screaming and shivering of metal, it toppled slowly into the sea and settled into the water.

"That was very clever," said Princess Lina, hanging onto the edge of the raft as it rocked wildly.

"Yes," said Hal, who thought it was too, and he reached over and patted the dragon, who was sending nervous puffs of smoke into the air.

"But it wasn't so clever to cut the rope," said the princess, hanging on even tighter. "The raft is coming to pieces."

Hal sighed and grabbed a tree trunk as the logs began to drift apart. It looked like the end for them this time. "Goodbye, Smoke," he said. "Goodbye, princess."

"Nonsense!" Princess Lina turned and gave Hal a push. "Into the sea!"

"What? We'll drown. There's no land in sight!" Hal clutched the logs desperately.

"The crab, of course. We'll get into the crab." She gave Hal another push that toppled him into the water, and jumped in after him.

"That crab's not alive," said Princess Lina, surfacing beside Hal. "It looks like one of those monsters the wizards make. They brought one to our castle."

Hal didn't answer. He just spluttered and started swimming.

The dragon, left alone on the disintegrating raft, cried piteously, and then, in desperation, flapped its wings frantically, and half flew, half swam after them.

Five or six strokes brought them to a giant metal pincer and they hauled themselves up into the opening. A metal tunnel sloped steeply upwards into darkness. The princess hardly hesitated. She grabbed a handhold and disappeared. Hal shrugged, took a deep breath, and followed her. Smoke, skittered on the metal and lumbered after him.

Hal climbed slowly up the handholds into darkness, trying not to think of what might happen next, and wishing for the hundredth time since this rescue had started that he had stayed at home and been apprentice to a butcher or a baker. All the talk at Hero School, all the lectures and lessons, had never even mentioned anything like monster crabs. He decided that school and the real world had nothing in common at all. All those years of sitting at desks, trying not to fall asleep, and listening to those retired heroes going on and on about honor and rules and the dignity of a hero had been a complete waste of time.

There was a twist in the pincer tunnel and Hal fell over a handhold and onto a soft pile of sea sponge.

"We're in the body of the crab." Princess Lina was sitting a few feet from him. Her voice echoed strangely.

"Hey! I can see!" Hal looked around slowly. A pale metallic light was filtering in from somewhere high above.

"There are windows in the crab's eyes," the princess said authoritatively.

"How do you know so much about it?" Hal was suspicious.

"Simple. I got a tour of the mechanical monster that came to the castle last summer. It's built on the same principle. I'm merely making a few inferences."

"Huh!"

"Never mind." Princess Lina was brisk. "Come on, let's explore."

She got up, but was immediately knocked down

again as the dragon tumbled over the last handhold and smacked her with its tail as it fell.

"Ah! Smoke!" She heaved the tail away.

"Aoo Ooo!" Smoke was all over them both, licking and crooning and making little smoke rings of anxiety.

They were in the middle of a round metal room, with ten metal tunnels at intervals around it. Set into the walls by each of the tunnels were heavy wooden levers. There was no furniture, just a few old blankets, a wooden bucket full of water, a cupboard full of dry seaweed, and some fish that smelt rotten.

"Someone lived here," said Hal, and he looked around nervously. "Do you think he's still around?"

Princess Lina shrugged. "There's no place to hide."

"No," Hal agreed. "It's a mystery." He leaned backwards with a tired sigh.

"Don't lean against that!" Princess Lina shouted at him.

Too late. As Hal's back rubbed against one of the levers, the lever moved sideways, there was a loud squeaking and rumbling, and the crab rocked from side to side.

Hal, the princess, and Smoke were hurled against a wall. The dragon puffed a smoke ring that had sparks of flame.

"Cut that out, Smoke! A fire is the last thing we need." Hal got to his feet and, holding onto the wall, which was now at an angle, he touched the lever gingerly. "So that's how it works. These wooden levers control the legs."

"And the pincers," Princess Lina agreed. "There's one lever for each of the eight legs and the two pincers."

Hal stared around the room. He could see now how the crab worked, but how could they see where to go? Surely there must be some way of directing the crab. His eyes rested on a round knob on the metal wall. That was it! He pushed on the knob and a sliding panel clicked open, exposing a narrow window slit. Morning sunshine flooded in and Hal, peering through the slit, could see the tree trunks from the raft drifting ahead of them, almost out of sight.

"Well," he said, suddenly cheerful. "We might be able to save ourselves after all."

"What do you mean *we*?" said the princess, staring out of the window beside him. "This was my idea. I had to push you off the raft, remember?"

Hal grinned. "All right. It was your idea and I'm glad you thought of it." He turned to the levers. "Now, let's see if we can make this thing walk."

Hours later, Hal had changed his mind completely about the crab being a good idea. He was hot, sweaty, covered in a black sticky grease from the levers, out of temper, and the crab had not made one single step.

They had pulled levers and pushed levers until

their arms ached, their spirits sank, and their ears rang from the screeching and clashing of the metal. The crab had tipped sideways, backwards, and round in a circle, as legs and pincers moved up and down. But they couldn't get it to move forward. Hal blamed the princess and the princess blamed Hal. Smoke slept through it all.

"If you could only try and keep time with me," Hal shouted in exasperation. "We have to get the legs going together."

"But you're not doing what I tell you," Princess Lina shouted back, wiping her black greasy hands on her dress. "I keep telling you and you don't listen."

In the end, darkness forced them to stop. They lay down exhausted on the sponge floor, and fell into an instant sleep.

Hal awoke to a grey early morning and a peculiar sensation on his face. It was Smoke licking him.

"Ugh!" Hal rolled over and pushed the dragon away. "Cut that out, Smoke!" The dragon crooned softly and butted Hal with its head.

"Ahh!" Hal screamed in pain. Smoke's spines were hardening fast into jagged bone.

"What's the matter?" Princess Lina sat up, stared around, and groaned. "I dreamed I was home in my own four poster bed and my servant was bringing me breakfast on a tray—fresh white rolls and butter and jam. But here I am in this metal crab. Starving, covered in oil and dirt and—" She stopped with a little sob, and examined her cut hands and broken fingernails.

Hal's stomach gurgled at the thought of white rolls and jam. He was very hungry, but the only things to eat in the crab were dried seaweed and rotten fish.

"All right," he said, standing up and stretching. "We'd better start again. We're going to starve for sure if we stay here."

"This time," said the princess, as she grabbed hold of a wooden handle. "This time, listen to me."

"Why should I?" he said. "You don't know how this crab works."

"Well, neither do you!" shouted the princess.

"That's true," Hal shouted back. "But I never saw a crab before. I don't know how they move their legs."

The princess stared back at him. "Oh!" she said. "That's it!"

"What's it?" said Hal, confused.

"Crabs don't walk forwards. They sort of scuttle sideways." She jumped to her feet. "We've been trying the wrong way."

"What do you mean?"

"Come on," said the princess. "This time it will work."

And it did. The crab walked. Not smoothly, or fast, but, lurching first one way and then another, it staggered sideways through the waves, across the sea.

"Lever one and two!" called the princess.

"Ready, steady, pull!" called Hal.

"Lever three and four!"

"Ready, steady, pull!"

Hour after hour went by. They stopped for a rest and a drink of water from the barrel and started again. The sun climbed high in the sky and turned the inside of the metal crab into a steam bath.

The black grease from the levers melted in the heat, and Hal and the princess became unrecognizable. Hal, turning to look at the princess, could hardly believe she was human. She looked, he thought, like one of the creatures from the inland swamps.

And then, squinting through the window slit, they saw a black dot in the sea ahead of them.

"It's the sea serpent!" said the princess, her voice rising to a scream. "I'd recognize that head anywhere."

"What shall we do?" Hal swallowed painfully as he remembered the poisonous breath and razor teeth. "We'll never escape!"

They stared at each other in panic for a moment— and then burst out laughing. They'd forgotten that the crab was much bigger than the sea serpent.

"The sea serpent will be scared of *us!*" said the princess.

Hal grabbed a lever. "Come on," he said. "Let's get it."

They sped up their rhythm and the monster crab

churned through the water, its giant legs crashing into the waves, the metal shrieking at the joints.

The gap narrowed rapidly and they could see the serpent rear its head to look backwards, its red eyes flaring in alarm.

"That's it! That's it! We've got it on the run!" Hal laughed. That sea serpent had a lot to answer for. If it hadn't taken the princess, he would be safe back at home.

"Now, let's move the pincers," Princess Lina said with relish. "That will really terrify it."

They grabbed the levers that worked the giant pincers, and the pincers snapped and clanged as they opened and shut above the sea serpent's head.

The serpent twisted and turned to escape, its neck almost wrapping itself into knots. The pincers came closer and closer, and then, just as they thought they had it cornered, the serpent dived beneath the surface and disappeared from view.

"Oh!" Princess Lina said regretfully, looking at the spreading ring of ripples. "It's escaped."

Hal grinned. "Well, I bet it's not going to stop for a long time. I don't think it will come around here anymore."

"I don't think it will ever—" the princess started to say, but she never finished her sentence. For, as she spoke, there was a noise like a thunder clap and the crab tipped sideways on its legs and crashed heavily into the water.

They had hit a rock. They'd been so busy chasing

the sea serpent that they had failed to see a faint blue haze turn into a rugged coastline, and had not noticed a line of jagged rocks protruding into the sea.

They pulled and pushed the levers desperately, but nothing happened. The rock had damaged the crab's legs. They were stuck.

"It's too bad," sobbed Princess Lina, giving up and throwing herself onto the sponge floor. "I recognize that coast. We're only a few miles from Castle Maze. But we might as well be a thousand. It's too far to swim ashore."

Hal cried a few quiet tears, too. And the dragon caught the feeling, and whined and lashed its tail around and blew smoke rings, until Hal and the princess choked and coughed and made it stop.

Then they sat still and said nothing for a long time. The only sound was the heavy breathing of the dragon as it napped, and the *whoosh whoosh* of the tide as it sucked and splashed under the legs of the fallen crab.

Hal heard the tiny squeaking noise first. He listened, and it grew louder. It seemed to be coming from somewhere under his feet. He put his head down to the floor. The noise was much louder there.

"What is it?" Princess Lina came over to him.

"Shh! Listen..." Hal started to say—when a part of the floor began to move upwards.

Hal and the princess stared as a trapdoor opened with a metal squeak and a small knotted figure crawled out.

Hal drew his sword.

"Don't hurt me," the figure croaked, and threw its arms over its head. "I'm Kale."

As the figure came into the light, they could see that it was a man dressed in rusty black, with a skin so wrinkled and folded it was hard to believe he was human. He could not stand upright, but hunched down with arms so long they almost reached to his feet.

"So, there *was* someone here all the time," said Hal, putting up his sword.

"Why did you try and attack us with the crab, Kale? And why did you hide?" Princess Lina said sternly to the cowering creature.

Kale bowed awkwardly. "I used to be a magician," he croaked slowly, as if talking were an unusual activity. "This crab is my invention. But it keeps going out of control. I didn't mean to attack you." He stopped and looked at the floor. "When I heard you climbing into the crab, I got frightened and hid."

"Well," said the princess. "Can you fix the crab so it will go again?"

Kale shook his head.

"That's that then," said Hal, and he paced restlessly around and around. "Prisoners in a broken crab."

Kale coughed. "I don't understand," he said shyly. "Why don't you go ashore?"

Sixteen

DRAGON DISASTER

"**I**t's too far to swim." Hal stared at the sea. And then he rubbed his eyes and stared again. Rocks were shining, wet and slippery, in the sunshine. The tide was going out, so that every minute more and more rocks were being uncovered, and great piles of seaweed were left to steam in the heat of the day.

"Hey! Hey! Hey!" Hal shouted, as he danced around and twirled on his toes. "We're saved! We're saved!"

Princess Lina jumped to her feet and ran to the window slit. "How? Is someone coming?"

"The rocks! Look!" Hal pointed. "The tide has gone down and we can climb along the rocks to the shore."

"Oh!" said Princess Lina, and she laughed, her teeth flashing through her grease-covered face, and clapped her hands. "I'll be home for dinner."

Hal turned to the hunched figure. "You'd better come with us to Castle Maze. You can't stay here."

Kale shrank backwards. "No. No. I am scared of people. I have lived in the crab for years."

"But the crab is broken," said Princess Lina. "You'll starve if you stay here."

Hal frowned. "I know a place you can go," he said. "There's a small hut and a pond with ducks, just around the bay. The girl who lived there has gone away. You'd be safe there."

"Oh, thank you." Kale clasped Hal's legs and bowed to the floor. "Oh, thank you, kind prince."

"Really!" Princess Lina shook her head. "He's not a prince. He's just a third-class hero!"

Hal banged on the postern gate of Castle Maze with loud, hungry thumps. Princess Lina and Smoke crowded impatiently on the narrow path behind him. They had climbed over the rocks and, after setting Kale in the right direction, they had walked along the cliff path to the castle walls—watched only by the hopeful goats who followed closely at their heels.

"Whadda you want?" an angry voice shouted from the other side. "Whadda ya hammering for?"

Princess Lina pushed Hal aside. "Open this door at once," she ordered. "This is the Princess Lina speaking."

There was a great laugh on the other side. Then the bolts were slid back with a clang and the door opened.

"Where's this princess?" asked the black-bearded gatekeeper, who poked a spear towards them.

"You'll pay for this!" snapped Princess Lina. "Let me in at once. My father will hear about you."

The gatekeeper choked and laughed at the same time. "I've heard everything now," he spluttered, waving the spear towards her. "A dirty filthy thing like you, a princess!"

"She is a princess." Hal stepped forward. "She is the Princess Lina."

"And you're a prince, I suppose!" laughed the man.

"I'm a hero," said Hal stiffly. "Don't you remember me? I saw you just last week."

"If you're a hero, then I'm the king of the world!" The man poked the spear at him. "Never saw you before in my life. You goat herders never know when a joke stops being funny. Now get back to your goats."

"Goat herder!" Princess Lina hissed. "How dare you! You...You..."

The door slammed in her face and the bolts rang.

"Well, what now, princess?" Hal said angrily. "Do we follow the goats?"

Princess Lina ignored him and pounded on the door with her fists. "Let me in! Open this door at once!"

But there was no answer.

"I don't understand it." She turned to Hal. "Why wouldn't he recognize me? Is the man mad?"

Hal stared at her thoughtfully. She was covered in mud and black grease from head to toe. She certainly didn't look the way she had when he'd found her, but then, was a princess only a princess if she looked like a princess? "Don't you have some kind of secret sign, a password or something?" he said finally.

"Of course not." Princess Lina tried tossing her hair, but then realized she didn't have any to toss.

Hal frowned. "What about a birthmark or six toes or something like that?"

"Do you mind? Are you crazy?" Princess Lina scowled. "I was born a princess. I don't have to prove it."

"Well, yes you do," said Hal. "That's just the point. Unless you can prove you're a princess, we're stuck out here with the goats."

"If only I could get to my father. He'd know it was me." Hal said nothing. He wasn't so sure.

The dragon chose that moment to make a swoop at a young goat who had ventured too close to its claws.

"Stop that, Smoke!" Hal yelled, and pushed the goat away. It baaaed loudly and joined its mother.

"There is one way I can prove I'm a princess," Princess Lina said. "I've just remembered."

"What's that?"

"If a true princess sleeps on twenty mattresses

and a pea is put under the bottom mattress, she won't be able to sleep. A princess has such sensitive skin she will be bruised all over by that pea."

Hal snorted loudly. "Obviously, you're not a true princess," he said. "You've been sleeping pretty soundly on the ground without even one mattress. Last night, you slept in a metal crab!"

Princess Lina sighed. "Yes. That's true. Some of the things I was told at Princess Camp aren't proving to be true at all."

"Same with me and Hero School," said Hal ruefully. "The only one of us who looks like what he is—is Smoke." The dragon was getting so big it would soon be safe from dwarves like Celti, who wanted to make dragon pie. The meat of a grown dragon would break your teeth.

Dragon pie! Hal gave a little whistle to himself. That was it!

"Open up! Open up!" He banged on the postern gate again. "I've got a dragon for Celti. He wants a dragon for dragon pie!"

A square peephole in the door was opened and the black beard of the gatekeeper showed through. "Shhh!" he said. "You'll have us all boiled in oil." He licked his lips. "A real dragon! Real dragon pie!"

"Yes," said Hal, pushing Smoke forward. "Here it is."

"Ahh!" The black beard moved forward. "I've only ever had dragon pie once, when I was a little boy, but you never forget!"

"Go get Celti," Hal ordered.

The peephole slid shut and there was silence.

Hal swallowed hard. He hoped his plan would work, otherwise poor Smoke would be...He tried not to think about what Smoke would be.

And then the bolts of the postern gate were pulled, the door pushed open, and Celti the dwarf bustled out.

"Who's giving me a dragon then?" he said. "Who are you?" And then catching sight of Smoke. "Ahh! What a beauty!"

"Celti!" Hal stepped forward. "It's me. I'm Hal, third-class hero."

"What's that?" said Celti, reluctantly taking his gaze away from the dragon.

"Hal, the hero who went after Princess Lina."

Celti stared hard at him. "You don't look much like him, but there is something about the voice."

"I've got a bit dirty I guess," said Hal. "But it is me, and my dragon."

"My! My!" Celti stared at him even harder. "Well, I guess it is. What a turnup." He stopped. "But why have you come back without the Princess Lina? Don't you remember the penalty for not finding her?" He cleared his throat. "Death by being pushed off the battlements!"

"But I have found her." Hal laughed. "Look!" He turned to the muddy figure beside him. "Here she is. Your Princess Lina!"

There was a strangled gulp from the dwarf as he

turned to stare. "No," he said finally. "It can't be."

"It is!" said Hal and the princess together.

"Oh, my!" Celti rubbed his eyes in horror. "Well, you'd better come in," he said doubtfully. "I guess the king had better see you."

"What about my dragon?" said Hal, as they entered the castle. "I don't want it harmed."

"Too bad." Celti took off his sash and tied it around Smoke's neck. "You shouldn't have offered it to me. A gift from a hero can't be refused."

Hal drew his sword and pointed the tip at Celti's throat. "Dragons are protected," he said fiercely. "Only a hero can kill a dragon."

"Unless the dragon is a gift." Celti backed away from the sword and rubbed his stomach happily.

The dwarf was right. Hal couldn't remember what number, but it was a hero rule. There was nothing he could do. Tears came to his eyes as he put up his sword and watched Celti lead Smoke across the courtyard and disappear in the direction of the kitchens.

Seventeen

END OF THE QUEST

"Never! Not my daughter! No!" King Maze closed his eyes in horror as Hal and Princess Lina stood before the throne and dripped black mud onto the marble floor.

"Yes I am, Father," Princess Lina said testily. "Of course I am."

"Don't look like her. Not at all." King Maze shuddered. "Like a mud ball." He shuddered again. "No princess dress. No princess hair. No princess!"

"You're being close-minded, Father," Princess Lina said angrily, and stamped her foot, spraying mud in all directions.

"No. No, I'm not." King Maze straightened his crown firmly. "Stands to reason. No crown, no king.

No armor, no knight. No uniform, no soldier." He stopped, breathless.

"A good point, Sire," said Celti, nodding. "Who would know a mother without a baby, a fisherman without a rod, or a chef without a hat?"

"No scales, no dragon. No bark, no dog. No stripes, no zebra." King Maze went red in the face, lost his breath, found it, and drummed his heels loudly against the throne. The guards stationed around the room banged the ends of their pikes on the floor in approval.

"Oh, really!" Princess Lina put her hands to her ears and Hal shuffled his ruined boots in dismay. It looked like back to the goats for them both.

"Well!" said King Maze, who had been made rather more good-humored by his speech. "All right, all right. If you're my daughter, what's your name?"

Princess Lina went pale. "My whole name?" she said weakly.

"Yes, yes!" said the king, settling back on the throne.

"What's wrong with that?" asked Hal.

Princess Lina took a deep breath. "It's not a name, it's an endurance test," she said. "Just you see." She cleared her throat.

"Hurry up, girl," the king snapped.

Princess Lina cleared her throat again. "I am the Princess Lina Sophia Esmeralda Belladonna Veronica Anastasia Angelica Evangelina Rosamunda Constantina Honoria..." She stopped, and took a gulping breath.

Hal was suddenly very happy to have only
name. What a memory you'd have to have for th
lot. But the princess wasn't finished.

"...Defender of the Dodo, Protector of the
Portcullis, Lady of the Lake, Mistress of the Moat..."

"But there is no moat, or portcullis," thought Hal,
as the princess took another breath. And how could
she defend a Dodo? It was extinct.

"...Keeper of the Keys..." Princess Lina's voice fal-
tered, "...and...and..."

"Yes? Yes?" said the king, leaning forward and
clutching his crown.

"...and...Heir to the throne of Maze," she finished
triumphantly.

There was a banging of pikes around the room.

"Quiet!" yelled the king. "Hmmm. What do you
think, Celti?" The dwarf consulted a piece of parchment he held in his hands. "Well, Sire, according to
my list, she has missed Guardian of the Gate and
Leader of the Lestinfryddd."

"What?" The king blinked. "What is Lestin...
dryd...did?"

Celti shrugged.

"Oh, yes!" Princess Lina snapped her fingers. "I
always forget those."

"She had better try again," said Celti.

"No." King Maze groaned. "Not again. Too
exhausting." He clapped his hands. "I know." He
turned to the princess. "Cut this short. If you're
Princess Lina, what was your baby name?"

Princess Lina scowled and went red in the face. "Do I have to say? It's so humiliating."

"Up to you," said the king.

"Oh, all right," the princess said. "Booboo."

"Booboo!" Hal grinned.

"Yes. Don't you dare say anything or tell anybody." She glared at him.

"Booboo!" The king roared with laughter, drummed his heels, and lost his crown over his right ear. "Booboo. That's right. Well, well. Welcome back, Princess daughter." He chuckled louder. "Won't kiss you. Too much mud. Have a bath."

"Food first," said Princess Lina.

"Very well," said her father. "And tomorrow, the wedding. Yes, wedding."

"*Wedding!*" Princess Lina shouted. "Whose wedding?"

"Yours, of course," said the king. "He signed a contract." He nodded at Hal.

Princess Lina turned to Hal and glared at him. "Well, he never mentioned it to me."

Hal went red in the face.

"We'll have to see about this," said Princess Lina, and she walked past him with her head in the air.

Hal turned to hurry after her and found himself next to Celti the dwarf.

"Congratulations on the rescue," said the dwarf. "Will you get promoted to second-class hero now?"

Hal didn't answer. He grabbed Celti by his tunic and shook him. "Where's my dragon?" he said.

"What have you done with Smoke?"

"Don't worry about it," said Celti, struggling to get free. "It's in the kitchen being stuffed."

"Stuffed!" Hal stared at the dwarf. "I'm going to..." He shook Celti harder.

"Remember the hero code of honor!" Celti's voice squeaked as he swung to and fro. "A hero can't go back on his word."

Hal let the dwarf drop to the floor. He had never felt so miserable in his life. His dragon was about to be made into pie, and tomorrow he was going to have to marry the princess.

The third-class hero was given an attic room in the very top of a tower, with a tin bath. Some servants brought him a new tunic (his old one was in rags). It was too big for him and had to be pinned at the back to keep him from tripping over it. But Hal didn't care. He picked at some food and sat looking out of the window slit, worrying about Smoke. What had seemed like a good idea had turned into a disaster. It would have been better to have stayed outside with the goats.

The door burst open and Princess Lina came in. She had on a long white princess dress, a gold girdle, a gold tiara, gold slippers, and her hair—her hair was long and golden and flowed down her back.

"But I cut your hair off!" said Hal, in surprise.

"It's a wig, dummy," said the princess, tossing back the curls. "Now, listen. I've come to talk to you about this wedding business. No offense. I mean, you're a nice third-class hero and I like you, but I want to travel and see the world before I settle down. So I'm very sorry to disappoint you, but I can't marry you."

"Well, I don't want to marry you either," said Hal. "But how do we get out of it? The contract said if I rescue you I have to marry you."

"I've got a plan," said the princess. "I can save us, but you'll have to trust me."

Hal looked at her doubtfully.

"We have to go down to my father now," she said. "I haven't time to explain. Just agree with what I say."

But it was a very worried hero that followed her.

King Maze was seated on his throne, and next to him, with a crimson cape and studded sword, stood a proper Hero! Gregory the Grey was a retired first-class hero, who toured the country judging promotions. He was beautifully dressed and you could see your reflection in his black leather boots.

"Hal, Third-Class Hero!" King Maze bellowed. "Come forward. Claim your reward. My daughter, the Princess Lina. Ring the bells. Ring the bells!"

Hal shivered in his borrowed tunic.

"But Father," said the princess, "I can't marry him because he didn't rescue me."

Hal was astonished. What did she mean, he didn't rescue her!

"You see," continued the princess in a sweet,

gentle voice, "I really rescued him, and that doesn't count, does it?"

"Why...er...no," said King Maze, puzzled. "No." He turned to Hal. "Well? True or not?"

So this was her plan, thought Hal. No wonder she hadn't told him ahead of time.

"Well?" said the king again.

"The Princess Lina...er...she did help me a little," said Hal.

"A little!" said the princess. "Why, if it hadn't been for me saving your life when the serpent poisoned you, you would have died. And if it hadn't been for me finding food and cooking it, we would have starved. And if it wasn't for my hair, we would never have been able to leave the island, and if it hadn't been for my plan, we would have drowned."

Hal shuffled his feet. "That's true," he said. "But—"

The princess interrupted him. "So you see, Father," she said reasonably, "it isn't fair to make me marry him."

King Maze nodded. "Quite right," he said. "Quite right." And he turned to Hal.

"Sorry, young man. Deal is off. No rescue, no wedding."

Hal was very glad about that, and he sighed with relief. But it wasn't fair about the rescue. The way the princess had talked, it sounded as if he hadn't done anything. Couldn't she have thought of a better plan than that? His cheeks flushed with anger.

Then the retired first-class hero cleared his throat, and everyone immediately fell silent. When a first-class hero spoke, even a king was silent.

"Hal, Third-Class Hero," he said. "You most certainly have a lot to learn. A princess should not have to cook, and as for cutting off her hair..." He stopped and raised his eyes to the ceiling. "That is terrible."

"I don't see why it's so terrible," said Hal crossly. "I can't see why a princess can't help out once in a while."

"Tut-tut," muttered the first-class hero. "I can see you have not been reading your Hero Handbook."

"Well, no," said Hal. "I lost it when the sea serpent attacked me, and then my dragon ate it." Thinking of Smoke brought tears to his eyes again, and he brushed them away.

The first-class hero tutted again. "Rule #107 states that the Hero Handbook must be on the person of a hero at all times." He fished in his tunic. "See?" And he held up his own handbook. "In all my career as a hero, I have never lost this—never."

Hal sighed. The Hero Handbook was all very well, but it was no use at all when you were being chased by serpents, eagles, and giants.

"And so," went on the first-class hero, "as Rule #37 states, no rescue, no promotion. You will continue as Hal, Third-Class Hero."

That was a blow. Hal sighed again. He was saved from having to marry the princess, but now he wouldn't get a promotion. It wasn't fair.

"I will now examine your sword," said the first-class hero coming forward, his own jewelled one glinting and swaying from a red leather belt.

Hal drew his sword from the scabbard and, kneeling down in front of the hero, he handed it to him, hilt first.

The first-class hero sniffed as he looked at it. Indeed, it was so rusty, blunt, and scratched that it hardly looked like a sword at all.

The retired hero removed the red memory jewel from the handle and held it up to the light. And instantly a picture flickered in the air.

As they watched, a picture of the dwarf Rolf's kitchen formed and the sword was shown toasting cheese by the fire.

"Toasting cheese!" The first-class hero said, amazed. "What sort of hero deed is that?"

The picture faded and another picture formed. This one showed the sea serpent's cave and Hal dangling upside down from the ceiling. As they watched, they saw the sword cutting the rope and Hal falling to the ground.

Hal blushed.

The next flashing picture showed the sword cutting off the hem of Princess Lina's dress, and the next showed it cleaning fish!

"Oh!" wailed the first-class hero. "Cleaning fish! A hero sword cleaning fish!"

Hal blushed again.

The retired hero didn't wait to see anymore. His

mouth was set in a very thin line and he snapped back the memory jewel and thrust the sword at Hal with a sniff of disgust.

"You'll be fined ten crowns for losing your Handbook, five crowns for unbecoming hero behavior, and five crowns for a new sword," he said. And he walked gracefully away, his crimson cloak swaying in the proper style.

Hal stared down at the floor. He was beginning to realize that what happened to you on a quest was not what the heroes wanted to hear about. They just wanted the rules obeyed and everything to be nice and tidy. But it wasn't nice and tidy out there in the world. And how was he going to get twenty crowns? He'd have to resign from the Hero union.

"Hal!" Princess Lina came and stood beside him. "Don't be angry. It was the only thing I could think of to save us from getting married."

"You could have told the hero how I saved you from being washed overboard on the raft and being crushed by the metal crab," said Hal, trying not to shout.

"I got the money from my father." She held up a small leather bag that chinked with coins. "I told him that you did help, so he gave me the money."

"I'd forgotten the reward," said Hal, grabbing the bag. "How much is it?"

"Twenty crowns," said the Princess.

"Twenty crowns!" said Hal, and laughed with relief, but then stopped abruptly as he remembered Smoke. What good was twenty crowns when his dragon was being turned into pie? There was only one thing to do. He ripped the hero badge off his tunic and threw it on the ground. He was through with the whole hero business. He didn't want to be a hero anymore.

"Come on." He grabbed the princess's hand. "Celti is making Smoke into dragon pie. We've got to stop him."

The kitchens were alive with activity. Scullions were rushing around with pots and pans, cooks were rolling yards of pastry, and the smell of onion and garlic filled the air. Hal's heart beat fast. Were they too late?

Just then, there was a roar from the far corner of the kitchen, and a cloud of blue smoke drifted towards them.

"Smoke!" Hal and the princess ran across the stone floor.

The dragon was covered with oil and herbs and lying tied to a great wooden chopping block. A butcher, wearing a blue and white striped apron, was raising a great meat cleaver into the air.

"Stop! Stop!" shouted Hal and the princess together. Too late. The cleaver swung down with a sickening *thwack!* Hal closed his eyes and turned away.

Thwack! Clang! went the cleaver, and the butcher howled in pain as the metal bounced off the dragon's skin and jarred his arm from wrist to shoulder.

A sigh went up from the watching crowd of servants.

"Look, Hal!" Princess Lina laughed. "Look. They can't cut through the skin. It's got too tough. Smoke has grown up!"

Hal opened his eyes and stared. It was true. The butcher was holding his arm and the cleaver was dented.

"No good now," said a chef with a tall white hat. "The flesh will be like rock. It would break all our teeth."

"What a shame," said a page in red and yellow livery. "I was looking forward to a bit of dragon. I've never tasted it." Smoke blew a few smoke rings, looked up at Hal, and grinned a dragon's toothy grin.

They said good-bye outside the maze. Hal had bought new red boots and a hat with a feather. Smoke had licked off most of the oil and been fed until he nearly burst.

"I want you to have this," said Princess Lina, and she pushed a small handwritten book into Hal's hands. "I made it myself. My writing's not very good." She looked at him doubtfully. "But it's all the dragon words. I thought you might like them to speak to Smoke."

"Thank you," said Hal. "I wish I had something to give you."

"I took a dragon scale off Smoke's back," said the princess. "One of the golden ones. Smoke wasn't too pleased. But I thought it would be a good souvenir. I'll wear it round my neck."

It was a lovely warm day, and Hal whistled as he walked along with his dragon waddling beside him. Being a hero hadn't turned out the way he expected at all. He was glad to be an ordinary person again. He didn't have to worry about any rules and he had money in his pocket.

"Well, Smoke," he said. "I have a thought to go and visit the Princes of Aristo and see what happened to them." He looked down at the paper the princess had given him.

"Aoaoaa ooo!" he said slowly.

Smoke stopped walking and gave him a look.

"Come on," said Hal. "I said walk fast in dragon. Aoaoaa ooo."

The dragon looked at him again in a puzzled way, and then slowly stood on its head, its legs waggling in the air. Hal sighed. He might have guessed that Princess Lina's instructions would have been mixed up. Goodness knows what she had written down. He gently pushed the dragon over and grabbed it by the neck.

"Let's go," he said, and pointed down the road.

And off they went.